NEW MONEY
—— *for an* ——
OLD AMERICA

Also by Frieda Dowler:

The New World Kingdom of Heaven

NEW MONEY
for an
OLD AMERICA

Frieda Dowler

iUniverse, Inc.
Bloomington

New Money for an Old America

iUniverse books may be ordered through booksellers or by contacting:

iUniverse
1663 Liberty Drive
Bloomington, IN 47403
www.iuniverse.com
1-800-Authors (1-800-288-4677)

Because of the dynamic nature of the Internet, any web addresses or links contained in this book may have changed since publication and may no longer be valid. The views expressed in this work are solely those of the author and do not necessarily reflect the views of the publisher, and the publisher hereby disclaims any responsibility for them.

Any people depicted in stock imagery provided by Thinkstock are models, and such images are being used for illustrative purposes only.
Certain stock imagery © Thinkstock.

ISBN: 978-1-4759-6739-5 (sc)
ISBN: 978-1-4759-6740-1 (ebk)

Library of Congress Control Number: 2012923559

Printed in the United States of America

iUniverse rev. date: 12/11/2012

. . . hope for the future is found in the past . . .

CHAPTER 1

I t was Monday morning, like any other weekday, but it would be the last of its kind for Wilma Smith.

Wilma pulled into the parking lot of Bledshaw Corn Products and Industries promptly at 6:30 a.m. Every work day, never one minute before or one minute after, but promptly at 6:30, she arrived to begin the day's business. As she walked to the building, she rummaged in her purse for the front door key and juggled a sealed coffee mug between forearm and side while dangling a lunch bag on her arm. She tolerated the inconvenience of the mug, not willing to start the day without two cups of her favorite blend. She always brought one from home to have while she brewed fresh at the office. Wilma made her mental calculations as she unlocked the door: *Mr. Bledshaw will be out this morning, so no need to make a full pot. Half a pot will do. One cup for me and two for Mark.* Mark was the sales rep for the company that produced the packaging used by Bledshaw Corn Products to ship their ground corn all over the world. Monday was the day of his weekly visit. She could handle the small challenges that might present themselves during the day. Everything was fairly predictable in Cedar Lake, Indiana. Predictability with two cups of coffee, just the way she liked it.

Wilma flipped the light switch just inside the door, dropping her keys in the shuffle. "I'll get you later," she said as she unloaded her purse, lunch bag, and coffee mug onto her desk just to the right of the main reception room. "First stop, coffee pot. Then keys." She rounded the tired brown leather sofa, opened the walnut cabinet that housed the coffee supplies, measured out the grounds and water, and turned on the coffeemaker. As the coffee began to brew, she retrieved the keys and turned on the remainder of the lights, except for those in Mr. Bledshaw's office. She closed his door, signifying to everyone he wasn't in. Otherwise the lights, open entry door, and the classical music wafting softly in the air told everyone, "You are welcome here."

Wilma's first order of business every day was to check e-mails. Deciding who needed what set the pace for the day. She perused the thirty e-mails and noted the priorities, and then allowed the aroma of coffee to lift her from her seat and set her humming towards the prize. As she poured her coffee, she heard a loud whir. Smiling, she noted the time. The machines on the processing side of the business always started at 6:45 a.m. and the crew began working promptly at 7:00. They were working through an abundant crop from last season, which would thankfully last them through this year's harvest.

Corny's, as the locals called it, employed 22 percent of the people in Cedar Lake. Processing and distributing corn meal worldwide was a third-generation family business, dedicated to its employees and the economic stability of the town, something of a dinosaur in the 21st Century. Years ago, the Bledshaw family saw the advantage of the regional crop. It met the steady demand of corn meal for a variety of uses. The company had steadily prospered, even during the double-dip recession of the previous decade. Their simple product, abundant in the Midwest, was milled, packaged, and distributed from the building in which Wilma now sat.

Twenty-five years earlier, Corny's had hired Wilma. Ray, her husband, had also worked at Corny's and retired five years ago despite Mr. Bledshaw's pleading. Ray was ready to take life a little easier. He remained on call whenever needed, but liked to putter around as the town handyman when he wasn't fishing on the lake in the summer and hunting in the winter. As Bledshaw's plant maintenance supervisor, he had been invaluable to the company's success as he kept spending at a minimum through his creative ways of running the physical plant.

Wilma was a matronly forty-three when she answered a *help wanted* ad in the local paper. She had no formal training in bookkeeping, but she managed the home finances, served as a trustee at the church, and helped organize the county fair every year. It didn't take Mr. Bledshaw long to recognize her talent and dedication. She became his most valuable asset, keeping the business profitable, although she dismissed his accolades as common sense.

With some effort, Wilma pushed open the vacuum-sealed door leading to the plant from the office side of the business. Her lack of strength was beginning to catch up with the matronly appearance she had maintained throughout the years. She knew everyone by name, but she had four long-time friends with whom she had lunch every day. Most mornings she greeted them as they came in. She spotted the four walking in together, all talking at the same time as she walked across the wide front aisle, framed by several rows of corn chutes suspended from the ceiling above work benches. All were dressed in the same tan work pants and tan shirt, belted at the waist, setting Wilma apart in her navy pants and red blouse.

"Hey, girls, how's the morning?"

"Oh, Suzi burned some banana bread she baked this morning," said Barbra Jean. "Now we don't have a treat with our coffee at break."

"I didn't hear the timer go off," said Suzi, defending herself.

"Oh, it isn't the first time," chided Margaret.

"I got distracted."

"What this time?" asked Jean.

"Birds," said Suzi.

"Birds?" questioned Wilma.

"Yeah, one of those Canadian geese got after me when I was watering the flowers. I tried to run him off 'cause I don't like dealing with his droppings. He nearly bit me and he put up so much racket I couldn't hear the timer even though I left the window open."

Everyone laughed but Suzi.

"I can just picture it: Suzi swatting that thing with the hose!" Barbra Jean cackled.

"It's not funny. They can draw blood."

The warning buzzer sounded. "Two minutes to clock in. You'd better get going," said Wilma.

As they hustled to the lunchroom where the time clock was hanging on the wall next to the refrigerator, Margaret called over her shoulder to Wilma, "Check those tickets this morning so we don't have to wait 'til Wednesday or Thursday. I heard on the news last night that somebody won the big jackpot."

"Oh, all right," said Wilma. "I'll see you at lunch."

Every week for the past ten years, the friends each contributed five dollars to buy lottery tickets, always purchasing them on Saturday night from the same convenience store. Each of them would drop off their five dollars to Suzi along with five numbers on Friday when they clocked out. They had a ritual of randomly choosing one of each of their five numbers by rotation; the power ball number would be the day of the month. They played $15.00 on the multi-state lottery and $10.00 on their own state lottery. Suzi always dropped the tickets off to Wilma on Saturday, but by Sunday they had forgotten. Casually, usually between Wednesday and Friday, one of them might ask Wilma if they had won. It was her responsibility to check the winning numbers on Monday.

Back in her office and ready to start checking off her task list, Wilma quickly forgot Margaret's request. She busied herself until almost ten o'clock when she remembered somebody had won the lottery. She went to her "Favorites" tab, opened the Hoosier Lottery website, and clicked the "Check Numbers" tab. "Guess I need the tickets," she said to herself. She slid her hand into the side pocket of her standard choice of purses for the past five years, retrieving the tickets without taking her eyes from the screen. One by one she typed the sequences of numbers. "Sorry, better luck next time" would flash until she typed in the next sequence.

Into the trash they went. But when she finished typing the final sequence of numbers, the screen went white. Wilma blinked and put her hands in her lap. Suddenly a red star flashed on the screen with big blue letters: "WINNER!"

"That can't be!" she said loudly and maneuvered back to the home page of the web site. She carefully retyped the sequence of numbers and received the same response. She put her hands to her face and shook her head. Wilma pushed back from her desk and stood. She paced around her desk a couple of times then sat again in front of the computer. This time she said the numbers aloud as she retyped them. Same response. She slapped her hand on the desk and shook her head. "Now what are we gonna do?" she shouted. *Think, Wilma, think. Oh! Johnnie will know.* She dialed him from her personal phone.

"John Minda. What can I do for you?"

"Johnnie, you gotta come *now*! Take this thing and do something with it! It's poison. We're just a bunch of old ladies who wanted to have a little fun. Now look what's happened."

"What are you talking about, A-Dub? Should I call 911?"

"No, Johnnie, we're not in that kind of danger! This is going to ruin everything. I don't want anybody to know about this. I'll have to tell the girls, but other than that I want this to be a secret."

"What happened?"

She took a deep breath and whispered, "We just won the lottery, Johnnie. I mean, big . . . $798,000,000!" She swept a wisp of gray hair from her forehead with the back of her hand.

Minda dropped the phone and in one brief moment, the Norman Rockwell life he had known as a boy in Cedar Lake disappeared. He scrambled to retrieve the receiver, as if grasping for his fleeting memories, and then regained his composure.

"Say that again, A-Dub. Did you say 798?"

"That's right Johnnie. I checked on the computer, just like I do every week, and that's what it says."

John pushed away from his massive desk, stood up, and gave a long, low whistle. He looked out across Lake Michigan, mesmerized by the glints of sun on the water that turned into diamonds right in front of him.

Wilma sighed, looking around her neatly organized office. The dated décor, the picture of the company's founder, family photos, even the trash receptacle had changed very little over the past twenty-five years. This was sure to catapult her life in a direction that was out of her control.

"Johnnie, I never really thought we would win. I'm not so sure this is a good thing."

"What do you mean, not a good thing? How can winning lots of money not be a good thing? Now you can be happy doing what you want for the rest of your life and not have to work at Corny's anymore."

"See what I mean? The poison is spreading already! Discontentment," she said, shaking her head. "I *am* doing what I want. Besides, didn't we teach you money can't buy happiness? Oh, it buys things but they only make you happy for a little while. You know our happiness has come from being a positive influence and helping others in Cedar Lake all these years. Now sitting here holding this winning ticket makes me realize everything's gonna change. Forever."

"You bet it will, A-Dub."

"None of us ever thought what would happen if we won. We just got into the silly habit of buying those tickets . . . and now look!"

"You mean you never had a fantasy about having lots of money?" he asked, directing the question more to himself. "I know I have, especially when things are tough. You know, kind of like a daydream escape."

"Maybe my life hasn't been as tough as yours 'cause I've never considered it. But maybe the girls have. We gotta get them together and figure this thing out. Anyway, I haven't told you yet, but we've all just applied to go live on The New World. Now I don't know what we'll do."

"Whoa, A-Dub. What are you talking about? The New World? You've never mentioned this. I can't believe you would leave the Cedar Lake you love."

"We were going to tell you and Jake in a few weeks, you know, homecoming week-end. But now this." Wilma shook her head again.

"It doesn't make sense for you to go to The New World, especially now. You're set for life with those winnings, and so are the girls. From what I've read, money and investments have limitations there."

"Johnnie, I'm 68 years old with a lot of life left in me. Your Uncle Ray, too. We've been in Cedar Lake since your mother died and we've loved every minute of it. But all the changes in the world are starting to affect Cedar Lake, too. The New World sounds like a place where we'd like to spend the rest of our days. Anyway, you and Jake have your own lives and don't need Ray and me anymore."

"We'll always need you, A-Dub."

"Oh, I'll miss you too, but if we don't go we'll only be a burden as we get older, and you know we don't agree with the new laws on euthanasia. I can't speak for the girls, but my guess is they're not gonna want that money either. That's why we gotta get together, tonight if you can come."

"Let me make a couple of calls to clear my schedule."

"I read on the Internet that someone should take charge of this ticket—put it in a lock box at the bank. But I can't do that around here. Everybody in town would know and I want it to be kept secret until we decide what we're doing."

"A-Dub, you just say what time." John chuckled. "By the way, I love that I'm forty-one years old and still call you that."

Wilma recalled when the twins began affectionately calling her A-Dub. "It makes me smile, too. I'm just glad everyone doesn't know the reason you changed it from Aunt Willy."

"Well, pubescent boys are likely to think anything is nasty," he said, laughing. "What time do you want me to come over?"

"Can you be here in time for dinner? I put a roast in the crock pot this morning. Oh, wait, I forgot you don't eat beef. Well, I can stop at Brown's Market and pick up a chicken breast. Won't take long to pan cook it."

"If I leave downtown by 3:00, I can avoid most of this Chicago traffic." John was scribbling on a note pad on his desk. He wrote 798,000,000 - 35% with a notation to the side: "taxes." "You know it takes about an hour if I'm lucky." He continued his scribbling: 518,700,000 ÷5 = 103,740,000. "But, yeah I'll be there for dinner. Ask the girls to come after that. I'd like to visit with you and Uncle Ray first. I'll be there around 4:30."

"Dinner is always at 5:00, so I'll ask the girls to come at 6:00."

"Got any sweet tea?" asked John, relishing the thought of a favorite childhood memory.

"Made some this morning. I'll let Ray know you're coming. Can't wait to see you. It's been just a little too long this time." Wilma hung up the phone and sat in silence, staring out the window. To her relief, with Mr. Bledshaw out this morning, and with Mark's visit already past, nothing demanded her attention—except her present dilemma. Wilma's involvement with the finances of Corny's gave her a proper perspective of money. People need it but if not treated sternly, it would rule them, like a spoiled demanding child. When treated properly, the outcome was order and respect. To Wilma, money was a means to an end. And the end, not the means, was the goal.

The Town of Cedar Lake had remained unaffected by the country's high unemployment. The country had plummeted into a double-dip recession from which it couldn't quickly recover while Cedar Lake prospered. Their economy did not depend on bottom-line driven businesses whose high cost of business and erratic strategies caused failures, leaving many unemployed. The town supported itself in a micro-economy based on its fair tax colony status, one of two that existed in the entire country. The town owned and incorporated land which it leased to businesses for ninety-nine years, renewable at the end of that time, while the citizens owned and maintained their buildings. The town became responsible for all taxes, which it collected from businesses with the lease; successive generations kept the family businesses going under the ninety-nine year agreement. Furthermore, chain stores were restricted by local government leadership who diligently protected jobs and supported local independent businesses. This system assured the economic stability of the town. The residents boasted a great deal of civic pride, and the town rallied to keep itself viable in spite of the severe economic collapse in the early part of the century.

Wilma headed out to the factory to ask the girls to come to her house at 6:00 that evening. She shoved against the air-vacuum door with her shoulder, expecting her help would make it open more quickly. She swiftly walked to Margaret's work area. Margaret, a woman in her mid-sixties, neat and trim, dressed in a tan work uniform, wearing a safety mask and brown gloves, was busily managing a twenty-five pound size burlap bag while a chute filled it with ground corn. She greeted Wilma with a smile.

"Hey, Margaret. Did you have a good visit with your new great-grandbaby?"

"Oh yeah. He's the cutest thing. He said his first word Saturday. It was 'cookie.'" Margaret pushed the stop button on the corn chute and eyed Wilma curiously. "I'm thinking you didn't come all the way out here to ask me about Evan. What gives?"

"Just wondering if you and the girls could come by tonight about 6:00?"

"What about The New World special? It starts at 6:00."

"Oh yeah, I forgot. Well, you gotta come at 6:00. We'll record it and watch it together."

"What's going on?"

"Oh, just got a surprise and want to tell you all at the same time."

"It's not a baby is it? Is Treeny finally pregnant?" Margaret started to clap her hands.

"No, it's not a baby. Just pass the word on to the others to come at 6:00."

"What if they can't make it?"

"Tell them they have to or I'll send Ray to get them."

"It's that important, huh?"

"Just make sure everyone is there," she whispered as she looked up and down the aisle and behind Margaret. Satisfied that she hadn't aroused anyone's curiosity, Wilma quickly turned to leave before Margaret could probe her any further.

Margaret glanced at the corn-dust covered clock hanging over the lunchroom door as the buzzer sounded signifying a break while the central corn grinder reloaded. She heard the machines turn off one by one. She finished filling the bag of corn and shut down the chute. She took off her mask and gloves, laid them under her workbench, and walked three aisles over to Suzi, stuffed into the same tan uniform and filling the same kind of burlap bag with corn.

"Hey, Suz, Wilma wants all of us to come to her house tonight at 6:00. Can you come?"

"What about the special?" said Suzi as she adjusted the chute, making sure the final bit of corn was hitting the bag.

"She said we could watch it together and that we all needed to be there. She has something she wants to tell us."

"Wonder what it is?"

"It must be important. She said she would send Ray to get us if we didn't come."

"I'm gonna come just to satisfy my curiosity."

"It's probably about The New World. That's all she and Ray are talking about these days. Anyway, can you pass the word along?"

"Sure, I'll tell Barbra Jean and she can tell Jean. I know how it works."

"See you tonight." Margaret turned and headed to the restroom.

NASSA (National Administration of Scientific Space Advancement) had kept The New World fabricated planet a secret until a specified time. Once they released the news, it immediately spread like wildfire as the hottest topic on the Internet, television, magazines, and newspapers. When they knew of its existence, the residents of Cedar Lake chatted wildly how something so monumental existed while they were living in their time warp. The man-made planet gave hope to a nation beset by a decade-long socio-economic revolution prompted by financial devastation. Major manufacturing entities, the backbone of the economy, exited the United States for cheaper labor and lower taxes elsewhere. Replacement jobs for middle income America though a national healthcare program provided many but did not come about quickly enough. The over-spent, out-of-work nation was left in a mess. The solution proposed by the National Disaster Relief Agency promised to eradicate one-third of the problem by creating an entirely new planet with jobs to sustain itself.

Ray, Wilma, and the girls had talked about other reasons, besides adventure, for wanting to live on The New World. The new laws in America increasingly opposed established values, and the free market system was slowly dying as society depended more and more on big government. They felt their freedom suffering a challenge they couldn't live with any longer. The New World promised that Christian values would continue to flourish, since those asked to volunteer were of that faith.

The new world beckoned to Christians as a Promised Land . . . a refreshing opportunity for this aging group of friends who were feeling more and more out of touch with this world.

CHAPTER 2

The sun-glint diamonds on Lake Michigan continued to tease at John Minda's imagination as he stared out the window on this clearer than usual morning. Working for this renowned global firm specializing in corporate investments on the 53rd floor of the John Hancock building was an accomplishment he had yearned for since entering the professional world. He was a valuable, insightful financial advisor and broker, and the firm had gladly provided him with a plush office suite and a staff to facilitate his business.

He looked at the hand-scribbled note he was holding and smiled. One hundred three million, seven hundred and forty thousand. He checked his watch: 10:25 a.m., Monday. He had a lot of work to do, and he knew his best defense against interruptions would be to focus on priorities and eliminate distractions. Pushing away from his massive mahogany desk, he silenced his phone and dropped it in the pocket of his suit jacket hanging in the closet on the way to his executive lavatory. He splashed cold water on his face and gave a long look in the mirror surveying his meticulous appearance. Grabbing a towel, he straightened his 6"2" frame and flexed his muscular chest. Taking in a deep breath, he spoke to the image staring back, "You've got a lot to do in the next five hours."

Back at his desk, he buzzed for his assistant. "Hold all my calls today. I mean all of them." He punctuated his request with an abrupt tone of voice.

"Mr. Minda, sorry but I do have an interruption that I know you'll want to take," said his assistant.

"It better be important."

"It's your brother's earning statements. I apologize, but you asked me to let you know as soon as they arrived. I just opened the morning mail."

John cleared his throat and in a gentler voice said, "Bring them in."

She put them in front of John and he began reading at the bottom. He pulled up Jake's account on his computer screen to access the full ledger. A quick estimation of Jake's assets registered at around $20 million. He spoke a voice command into his phone, "A-Dub at work."

She answered, "Cornelius Bledshaw Industries. May I help you?"

"A-Dub, it's me again. Can you do me a favor when I come over tonight?"

"Sure, Johnnie. What is it?"

"Can we *not* talk about Jake again?"

"Well, I suppose. I did want to talk about homecoming weekend. You and Treeny are still planning to come, aren't you?"

"Yes, we're coming. I just don't want you to think that any of this lottery money will fix his problems, because it won't. And I know you and Uncle Ray well enough that you'll want to make sure that he has a fair share of it."

"You're right, we will. The way he lives, well, we just don't understand it. A little money might make things better for him."

"I handle his investments and his living allowance, so I'm telling you he's okay. Having enough money is not his problem. Having enough brains, that's the problem."

Aunt Wilma interrupted sternly, "Johnnie, don't talk about your brother like that! He's made some mistakes, but he's still your brother."

As fraternal twins, both Jake and John were handsome, charming, and determined. But that's where their similarities ended. Jake inherited strong Navajo genes from his father in appearance as well as inherent qualities. John favored his mother with olive skin but his father in bone structure with high cheek bones and chiseled jaw. Their views of life differed as much as appearance and their outlooks took them in opposite directions. From an early age, John accepted the loss of both their parents, and allowed A-Dub and Uncle Ray to be their substitutes. Their parenting, with clear boundaries and a lot of love, was what he needed to be successful in life. He respected himself, and so had genuine respect for others. He was congenial, trying hard to be helpful and showing kindness to others, mainly because he recognized it benefited him in the long run. John observed Jake's behavior throughout high school and felt obligated to apologize for him, thinking he himself would be judged by Jake's actions. He wanted people to know they were different.

Jake, disappointed and angry over his losses, withdrew. He challenged everything and everyone he came across, determined to be tougher than the pain that wracked his soul. He pushed boundaries beyond limits, even when it meant destroying himself and all of his relationships. He had no respect for himself or anyone else and sought attention through defiance. Jake recognized John's ulterior motives behind his "Mr. Nice Guy" exterior and had no respect for him because of it.

Jake had been a football star in high school, a big deal in Cedar Lake. He excelled at the sport and attended Purdue University on a full-ride athletic scholarship. While there, he caught the attention of the National Football League and was recruited to play professionally immediately after college graduation. But in his fifth season in the NFL, he sustained a closed-head injury that brought about his early retirement. His multiple brain bleeds were too risky even for state-of-the-art laser surgery. Though the body would eventually absorb the blood, leaving time to heal the wounds, progress was slow . . . almost nonexistent. He needed scans every three months to determine how he was healing. Jake felt the doctors only gave him hope to keep him on a level mental keel. His physical activities had to be kept at a minimum, and since he had never exercised much of his brain, determining how his thinking process was affected was difficult. Jake was emotionally driven, so when the football train crashed, his emotions careened him on a three-year ride because he had no other plans for his life. After his sixth brain scan, he turned to the bottle to escape the multiple levels of pain and wait it out. A-Dub warned him he might turn out like his father, but Jake was convinced his drinking was under control.

John had begun investing wisely for Jake after his third season of pro football. Jake wasn't interested in knowing about his investments . . . as long as he had enough to support his irresponsible lifestyle. John doled out a living allowance, hired a bookkeeper, and generally accommodated Jake's additional requests for cash.

John, however, advised against Jake's financial venture three years after his injury. Jake decided he needed to find an identity other than football, so he returned to the heritage of his ancestors. He moved to the Navajo Nation in Arizona where the family name gave him rights to 120 acres of undeveloped land. Sixty acres came from his great-great grandfather's family and 60 acres from his great-great grandmother's family and since John had no interest, Jake claimed it all. He petitioned the Tribal Council—and greased some palms—for permission to build a convenience store, gas station, pizza pub, and coin-operated laundry all under one roof, between the towns of Chilchinbito and Kayenta near the Black Mesa. Even though alcohol consumption and sales were prohibited by Navajo law, he found a way to bootleg it by partnering with high-ranking officials.

Jake named the place Gravely's Gulch, and adorned it as a shrine to his football hero—himself. He lined the walls of the pizza pub with photos, articles, and trophies. He selected a business partner, a Frenchman named Louis Gravél, whose only investment was his time, to run the establishment. Louie had managed the luxury hotel lounge in Dallas where Jake hung out after he started drinking excessively. Louie fooled nearly everyone, including Jake, with his proper ways. He was not, however, without his own agenda, and in the long run, it paid off. Louie got his name on the big sign, kept his fingers in the till, and helped see to it that Jake got drunk—every day.

Jake's enterprise started ten years earlier. John was concerned Jake would spend all his money and leave himself with nothing. But to John's surprise, Gravely's made money—hand over fist—despite poor bookkeeping and Gravél's sticky fingers. The Navajos needed what Jake had brought them; they spent what little money they had and all their time at The Gulch, which became their preferred gathering place. In a codependent return on investment, Jake's desperate ego was stroked by his persuasion with the Tribal Council and the police, elevating him to an attention-getting status much like that of football hero. He soon discovered that not only did football buy influence, but so did money.

John had established all of Jake's investment accounts, and in the obligatory stack of paperwork, Jake signed a document naming John as the sole beneficiary of his investments. John purposely had not mentioned this to Jake and Jake had never considered a beneficiary.

John logged out of his computer four and a half hours later and neatly organized everything in stacks on his desk. He looked at the time. It was 2:30, earlier than he expected. He buzzed his assistant. "I'm leaving for the day. There are some things on my desk that you'll know what to do with. See you tomorrow."

"Is there anything else, Mr. Minda?"

"No, that's it for today. By the way, are there any calls I need to return before I leave?"

"You've had seven or eight, but nothing urgent. I think they can wait until tomorrow. Treeny called though."

"Thanks. See you tomorrow."

John, in order to avoid delays caused by conversations with co-workers, made his way through the back door of his office to the service elevator, took a walkway to another set of elevators, and emerged at his rooftop parking space. As he stepped outside, the air enveloped him like sheer gauze and the gentle breeze fanned the warm sun on his face. He took a deep breath and exhaled his responsibilities.

It was a perfect June day. John couldn't recall a better one. He opened the door to his Mercedes CKL550 with fingerprint identity. He reminded himself why he had chosen the color white, to support his good guy image. He also chose this particular model because it was a proper image for him at a time when hybrids ruled the road. The $64,000 sticker price was considered modest by his colleagues. The fuel efficiency ratings implied some concern for the environment, and the sporty lines announced that he was willing to take calculated risks. His dream was to own a McLaren V-12 and max it out at 206 m.p.h., in spite of fuel rationing. Black, cordovan leather interior, aluminum alloy wheels . . . *Maybe soon I'll have my chance,* John thought.

As he exited the parking garage, he silently cursed the circular ramp, and wondered how many more times he would drive it. He and his wife, Treeny, enjoyed a big-income lifestyle despite society's trend toward minimalism. He had been blessed with the ability to make money and as long as the government didn't continue to confiscate more of his profits, he intended to fully enjoy the fruits of his labor. But some days the stress of the pace got to him, especially during the past decade when investments declined, causing some of his investors to lose hundreds of thousands of dollars. He was steadily tiring of juggling investments and sales all day and trying to spend enough time in each relationship to pacify his many clients. Some days, he just felt empty. He knew these relationships were based on what he could do for the other person and how much money it would make. He longed to be himself. That's what he loved about his visits to Cedar Lake. No one cared what he could do for them. To everyone there, he wasn't a 41-year-old, world-traveled financial wizard; he was just "Johnnie".

John flipped the lever to put the top down on his car as he headed toward Interstate 94, then activated the voice command button on his phone. "Call Treeny."

"Hey, babe. How's your day?" John said cheerfully.

"Oh my gosh, Johnnie, I've been trying to reach you all day. Didn't you get my messages?"

"Sorry, babe, I didn't. It's been a crazy day. I'll tell you about it later. It's been so crazy that I need a Cedar Lake fix and I'm heading to A-Dub and Ray's for dinner."

"Aw, been that rough, huh?"

"Yep, but A-Dub asked me to come. She needs some advice on something, and you know this is how I unwind."

"Well, I had something really cool happen and I wanted to talk to you about it. But if you've had a crazy day, then you need to clear your head. You don't need your crazy wife babbling about crazy stuff. I'll tell you tomorrow. Maybe we can have dinner at Cozy's?"

"What happened? I want to know," said John.

"I don't want to tell you on the phone," Treeny giggled, "but I can't wait." Her voice lifted as she continued, "I've been trying all day to come up with a match for a blue color that I saw in a dream or vision or something that happened to me this morning as I was waking up. I saw the tiniest angel on my bedside table dressed in the most incredible blue. It was sort of like an aqua-, sapphire-, turquoise-, sky-kind of reflective blue. It was beautiful, a color I've never seen. Imagine that, a new color! I want to match the color before I forget it. I can see my whole spring-summer line with bits of that blue in everything. I think it was a gift from above. And I can't tell you what it did for me to see that angel!" She paused, giving John a moment to respond, but he was silent.

The excitement in her voice dropped as she continued, "You know I've been asking God for a child again." A tear welled up in the corner of her eye. "Oh, I'm sorry, Johnnie. This is too much to do on the phone."

"Want me to come back and take you to dinner tonight?"

"No," Treeny said quietly. "These feelings aren't new. They're just the same old ones. She paused. "I'm sorry, I'm sorry. I don't want to ruin your drive to the country. This can wait until tomorrow. Tell A-Dub and Uncle Ray I love 'em and I'll see them in a few weeks when Jake comes. See ya when you get home and we'll talk about it tomorrow at Cozy's."

"Are you sure you're okay? You know you're more important to me than anything else."

"Yeah, I know. And you are to me, too. Really, I'm okay."

Johnnie loved his wife, and even though this relationship required more of him than any other, it was the one he valued most. This one was based on matters of the heart, not the rise and fall of the dollar. This one he was in control of and he was determined to make it work. He and Treeny shared the same values, but also respected each other's differences. Their priorities were God, each other (though sometimes those two got reversed), family, and work. They had developed these ideals through premarital counseling and ongoing marriage workshops and seminars. They had purposed to make this work "until death do they part."

Treeny was John's beautiful princess. She was 21 years old when he married her; he was 29. Eight years was a big age difference to most everyone they knew . . . but not to them. She was mature and mannered, and she could keep up with his circle of friends and acquaintances. She kept him grounded, and he called her an "old soul". She saw spiritual matters very clearly and kept him balanced. She was more interested in people than success. That was, of course, what made her successful. Everyone loved her in return and helped her achieve her dreams.

She was a boutique owner and a designer of baby clothes. Her label was "Treeny's Teenies," the hippest, hottest fashions for babies and kids up to age four. But despite her success in business, she was unfulfilled. She had suffered several miscarriages throughout their 12 years of marriage, all in the very early stages of pregnancy. Her doctor discerned no medical reason for her miscarriages, and suggested out-of-womb fertilization. They tried that two times. Still no babies. She developed a driving passion to design children's clothing to help keep her hope alive. Each day she focused on babies through her fashions and exhausted herself, working long hours, to numb the pain of her disappointment. She questioned God, but only in her darkest, most intimate thoughts. She convinced herself that He gave her this business as a substitute and determined to be satisfied with that.

CHAPTER 3

John Minda took the Bishop-Ford Freeway south out of Chicago, navigating the moderately heavy traffic and closely watching for East Bemes Road, then to Calumet and onto West 135th Street. Exiting onto a two-lane blacktop, he inhaled the country air and exhaled the tension of city traffic. He reveled in the landscape, the fresh green leaves on the trees, newly planted fields . . . and with every breath, he savored the fragrance of dirt mixed with manure. This was his catharsis, the part of his Nayajo heritage that refused to let go of him. Nature reminded him that the frenzied pace of the life he had built in the city, just a short one-hour drive behind him, was a world away.

As he passed Charlie Trotter's farm, he gripped the steering wheel and struggled to look away, as if sirens were luring him. He would have avoided going by it if there were another route to Cedar Lake. He accelerated in order to outrun the punishment of his memories, but quickly gave into the pain as though it would recompense for the loss of a life.

Mr. Trotter's barn and Selena Owens were also a world away, even though the memory remained just under the surface. John's brother Jake had jilted Selena, his girlfriend of two years, a couple of weeks before homecoming night, telling her they would probably go their separate ways after high school anyway and he wanted the freedom to enjoy his senior year in the company of anyone he chose. John had taken her for a ride to comfort her while the town turned out to worship Jake after he scored the winning touchdown. John never acknowledged the jealousy he had of his brother, but that night he came close. John reminded himself: "*People admired me too, just in a different way. I didn't play football, but I tried hard to do all the right things in life. I was respectful, mannerly, and helpful. That was my intention with Selena that night in Mr. Trotter's barn. I was only trying to help her over the breakup with Jake.*"

John saw how much trouble Jake and their father had caused, and he never wanted to be a burden to others by misbehaving. Jake welcomed all the attention his antics brought, whether for reckless driving through the center of town or for spray-painting graffiti on the town's water tank. The graffiti had been his prediction for the final score of the semi-state game their junior year and he had been right. The team went on to become state champions and Jake's excused misconduct became legendary. That made John furious and caused the tension between them to mount during the summer between their junior and senior years. Regardless, on that homecoming night, his only intention was to console Selena.

John bore down on the accelerator, ignoring the speedometer which registered 110. He could see a mile ahead on the straight flat blacktop, so he opened it up. He began arguing with himself as the sound of the engine drowned out the words.

"My frame of mind the night I took that drive with Selena was to comfort her. I was *not* using her to get even with Jake! But why else would I have done that with her in Mr. Trotter's barn?" *Where's this coming from?! I've asked God to forgive me for the abortion. Why does it continue to be so painful? Why can't I forget it?*

He shouted above the roar of the engine. "I give to the church faithfully and serve on all the committees I can! I'm always there when the doors are open! Sometimes I feel I don't have a personal life because of the volunteer work Treeny and I do at church!"

Screaming at the top of his lungs, he asked, "What else do I have to do?"

Out of nowhere, in broad daylight, a deer leaped across the road in front of John. He jerked the steering wheel to avoid a collision. The car swerved and the tires squealed as he struggled to maintain control. He slowed down and pulled off to the side of the road. Sweat beaded up on his forehead as he sat in the cloud of burning rubber. Opening the door, he glimpsed the white tail of a doe as she gamboled over a small rise in the distance. He walked around the car, kicking at the tires and swearing under his breath.

He shouted at the clouds. "Is that why Treeny can't have a baby? Are You punishing me? I only paid for the abortion! I didn't commit the murder!" Tears started to well up in John's eyes, but he took a deep breath and spat one more comment skyward. "Treeny doesn't deserve this!"

Ignoring the urge to continue his tirade at the clouds, he got back in the car and tromped the accelerator, leaving Charlie Trotter's barn, Selena Owens, and his guilt in the distance.

"Okay, get control," he commanded himself. "You can handle this." He flipped open the notepad lying on the passenger seat. He glanced at the hand-scribbled note he had attached with a paper clip to the first page of the legal documents he had brought with him. "The New World, huh? They're not going to need this there." He smiled, driving toward his future.

Even though parts of his childhood were unpleasant he was thankful that most of the time as a kid he felt loved and cared for. But his heart never stopped aching to know his mother. And he longed to know his father in any way other than as the drunk he had become. His mom's death and his dad's bottle had made this impossible, though, and eventually he came to accept that. A-Dub and Uncle Ray were the best substitutes he could imagine. A-Dub threw birthday parties, baked cupcakes for his classes, and attended every school event. Uncle Ray was knowledgeable about everything from woodcarving to oil changing, passing his knowledge along to John as they spent time together. Jake, on the other hand, figured out things by himself as he spent time alone on the fishing boat in Cedar Lake. Despite all of the attention he drew from his football career, Jake was a loner.

That the twins descended from the Navajos was evident not only in their physical features but also in their inherent respect of nature. Their great-great grandfather and great-great grandmother were both Navajo. The story told to them was their great grandfather married a Mexican girl, much to the disdain of his Navajo parents. As prejudices arose, love had its way and the young couple left the reservation. Great grandmother's clan, living in northern Arizona, welcomed them. Their grandfather was born as an only child. As he grew into manhood, he established a reputation for being a womanizer and never settled down with their grandmother. Instead, he left her with Jake's and John's father while he moved around the country. He did have the decency, however, to return her to the Navajo nation and build them a home on the sixty-acre family plot near the Black Mesa in Arizona. Then, he roamed, looking for work, building this or that, and sent his family what money he could.

When the twins' father, Juan, grew to be a man, he swore he would love his wife and take care of his family. He didn't want to abandon his children the way he had been. Determined to provide his family a good life, he left the reservation in search of steady employment. The ways of the reservation had changed very little in 200 years, causing the unemployed to outnumber the employed. Juan found work with a railroad in Chicago. There he met his wife, Jackie, a waitress in the coffee shop where he had breakfast every morning. Juan's life in downtown Chicago made him long to raise his family on the land. That's when he discovered Cedar Lake. It was southeast of Chicago, yet it was close enough to commute to work. His Navajo roots were satisfied as he fished on the lake in the summer and trapped in the winter. Jackie loved the country too as she developed domestic skills that benefited the family.

The twins were born into a time of national economic and social chaos, but Juan and Jackie's lives were unaffected as they sought peace in Cedar Lake. They enjoyed a love greater than any Hollywood movie could depict. Then one miserable, cold winter Jackie got sick and by early spring her young life was cut short by lung cancer. The family had no time to prepare emotionally for their deep loss. The twins were seven and too young to fend for themselves but that would become necessary. Juan Minda continued to work every day, but every evening he stopped at Sonnies', the local tavern, and hoisted a drink to help him cope with going to a home without Jackie. One drink turned into two, two turned into three, and soon he lost count. He couldn't face life without Jackie. She had been the one to care for the twins and he didn't know what to do with them or how to be a father and a mother. He was trying to escape his own loss at the expense of his sons. That year they lost both their mother and their father.

Jackie's sister, Wilma Smith lived with her husband, Ray, on the south side of Chicago. After Jackie's death, they drove to Cedar Lake every weekend to check on Juan and the twins. In late September, when the boys didn't start school on time, Wilma and Ray knew they needed to be closer to help. They had approached Juan's neighbors, shortly after Jackie's death, about buying their house. Initially they refused but by fall Ray's more than generous offer was accepted, so Wilma and Ray took on the care and feeding of a family of three, with two properties to maintain. Juan's self-destructive choices added to their burden. Taking on the twins was a delight that overshadowed the burden because Wilma had been unable to conceive during their ten years of marriage. Juan kept promising to stop drinking and help more with things, but the alcohol tightened its grip on him as an addiction from which he couldn't recover. Fifteen years of nightly consumption of nearly a quart of alcohol led to the failure of his health. He was never able to keep his promises. The twins were disappointed when he didn't come to school events. They assumed he didn't care; he assumed he was an embarrassment. As time went by, Juan burned the bridge between him and his boys. His death relieved everyone. His boys gave him a dignified funeral, but they missed him long before then.

John decelerated when the town sign came into view. He was early enough to enjoy a drive around the town square, and he wanted to savor good memories. The town center, just under a mile square, stretched for five blocks in each direction. The stately red brick courthouse with limestone lintels above the wide windows, the town offices in the same red brick, and a museum dedicated to the history of this fair tax colony were clustered in the center block. These served as the town's architectural centerpieces and were built as constant reminders of Cedar Lake's legacy and principles.

John drove past Nick's Candy Shop. The red and white circus-like striped metal awning had been kept pristine. His mouth watered for an orange phosphate from the soda fountain he loved. Most of the people he knew in Chicago had never heard of such a thing, but the ingredients were handmade and the recipe passed from generation to generation. Whenever John came to Cedar Lake, he felt as if time stood still while the rest of the world had advanced into the 21st Century, and for good reason.

In the late 1800s, the state government granted a fair tax status to a group of devotees of the philosophy advocating governmental leasing of land rather than private ownership. Their belief was that man should own everything he created, but the land belonged to God. The town collected appropriate rent for the land upon which private buildings stood; this rent funded the operation of the town. Every seven years, the town board would refigure a budget and, if necessary, assess a new rent. At the end of twenty-five years, any money remaining in the town's account after all budgetary items were satisfied, was redistributed to its citizens. Economic productivity was stimulated as the citizens anticipated their stipend by being responsible and productive. The more businesses there were to share in the operations budget, the less rent each would owe, and there was always hope of a refund. This financial arrangement also encouraged the citizens to act as watchdogs over the town board's spending decisions. The town not only became a lovely place to live, it also became a destination for tourism and curiosity seekers. The business owners welcomed them and enjoyed the extra revenue.

John meandered down Fairhope Avenue, lined on each side by a row of massive elm trees. The road was narrow, as the trees had been planted when there wasn't much traffic and cars were smaller. The trees had grown to more than twenty feet and formed an enchanting canopy overhead. The roots of the trees buckled the historic brick paved road, slowing traffic to a crawl. The storeowners along the avenue took full advantage of the situation, and generated sights, sounds, and aromas to entice buyers. The bait nearly persuaded John to stop for a bouquet of Treeny's favorite flowers, then he caught sight of the First Baptist Church. Something lured him that way instead.

Chapter 4

T
he sight of the church drew John like a moth to a flame quickly dispelling thoughts of a phosphate at Nick's or flowers for Treeny. The church sat with stately presence on Fairhope Avenue, two blocks from the courthouse in the heart of town. Massive white columns, across the red brick façade, bookended a wide set of concrete stairs leading to an exquisite set of hand-carved double doors. John's memory summoned the story about those doors, recalling that an old man had chiseled the Last Supper into the wood. No one knew where he came from, nor did anyone see him after he was finished. Many people believed him to be an angel. John himself had believed that as a child, but as an adult, he rationalized the story.

Growing up, John had spent every Sunday, Wednesday and two weeks every summer at day camp dedicated to learning the ways of God at the First Baptist Church. He had been baptized when he was ten, but by twelve was looking for excuses to play hooky from church. He began to think church was for old people who didn't want to have fun anymore. He and Jake both lost interest in church in their early teen years, preferring the outdoors to sitting in a building where the preacher gave them ample reason to daydream. John, out of a sense of duty, attended church more than Jake. When John married Treeny, they made going to church a priority. Her parents raised her as an Episcopal and John decided the formal structure of the service suited his dignified life more than a Baptist church. Anyway, he reasoned, there were no Baptist churches in downtown Chicago, where they chose to reside. Joining St. Mark's was a prerequisite to using the church for their elaborate wedding, so John agreed to attend.

Treeny grew up in a very traditional home with mannerisms indicative of old money. John recognized those from the start, and knew Treeny and her family were the kind of people he wanted to associate with the rest of his life. His challenge was convincing them he was worthy. Heritage was essential in her social circle, but he had no family legacy and no money, only a promise that he was on his road to making lots of it. He quickly proved himself a suitor of outstanding character and the family was delighted to accept him. He made Treeny happy, and that was their main concern.

She was born Katrina Louisa Collette, but fondly known as Trina. Her married name of Trina Minda was too sing-songy, so John began calling her Treeny, and the name caught on. She had set her sights on the world of fashion. Her parents had encouraged her to cultivate her creative gifts in art and design by sending her to summer camps, taking her on visits to the art museums on Sunday afternoons, and eventually enrolling her in the Fashion Institute in New York.

During her senior year, while she was home from New York on Christmas vacation, she met John at a gallery opening. It was love at first sight for both of them. Their courtship lasted a year and a half. Deciding to marry after six months of dating, they endured the proper one-year engagement. They would have eloped, but, naturally, her parents insisted on an elaborate wedding, bribing them into compliance with a two-week honeymoon in Hawaii.

John drove slowly past the church, rounded the block, came up the back alley, and slotted his car into a space in the asphalt parking lot. He walked around the side of the building and into the meditation garden. He lingered, deeply inhaling the sweet fragrance from the assortment of roses in the flower bed. It was an annual project of the women's group at the church for as long as he could remember. He glanced next door at the parsonage, wondering about Pastor Charles. He stopped at the reflective pond, recalling the last time he had been there. It was after Selena

Owens had informed him of her pregnancy. He shook off the memory and hastily moved on, stopping for a moment at the front of the church to take in its beauty. He noticed how well the church members had taken care of the building and the property. The small lawn was neatly trimmed and the sidewalks were immaculately edged. Under the weeping cherry trees, the flower beds were decked in red, white, and purple blossoms, providing an aesthetic balance on either side of the steps. He walked up the stairs to take a closer look at the doors, remembering his vow as a boy: *Someday, I'm going to make something special out of wood.*

He noticed one door was slightly open. He grabbed the bronze handle and pulled the massive door open. He expected the aged wood vestibule to be dark, but it shone with a cozy hue from the sun streaming through the stained glass windows flanking the deep hallway. One window depicted the manger, the other one, the cross. As the smell of roses permeated the air, he noticed a fresh bouquet on the library table where the bulletins lay. The doors to the vestibule were open, and John peered into the sanctuary. He stepped over the threshold into the sanctuary with golden colored walls and a beam of light struck him as it streamed in from a small octagon window high above the podium. He felt the warmth envelope him. The light drew him into the sanctuary and broke into his spirit, stirring his emotions by something he couldn't explain. He slid into a pew, bowed his head, and waited for a few minutes with his head down and eyes open. Then he noticed a shadow in the aisle beside him. Startled, he jerked his head to look, expecting to see something angelic. Instead, he saw Pastor Charles. The kindly clergyman had aged considerably, but John immediately recognized him.

"John Minda," said Pastor Charles tenderly as he smiled. "I've been waiting a long time for this moment."

"Pastor Charles, it's good to see you, too," said John. He stood and offered the pastor his hand.

Instead of shaking his hand, Pastor Charles embraced John with a hug. "I've prayed for you every day for the last twenty-three years."

John stiffened, nervously clearing his throat. He couldn't recall a time when he and Pastor Charles had embraced, but he knew an aging man could be sentimental. The hug seemed like it would never end and John was relieved when Pastor Charles backed up to give him a look.

"Where are you headed, John?"

"I'm going to A-Dub's and Ray's for dinner."

"No, John—not your destination today, what road are you taking in life?"

"I guess you would say," John looked to the floor then back to Pastor Charles, "I'm taking the road to success. God has gifted me with the ability to invest well and profit generously." John cocked his head and smiled.

Pastor Charles folded his arms across his chest and patiently nodded his head as John continued. "I've got a great wife who loves me and she's gifted artistically. Her line of children's clothing is very popular. Our church life at the Episcopal Church in Chicago dominates our Sunday mornings and we are faithful with giving. We enjoy about anything we desire."

Pastor Charles looked intently into John's eyes. "John, I know your circumstances. I've kept up with you through Wilma and Ray. What I want to know is, are you seeking peace and contentment?"

John shifted onto one foot, cleared his throat, and politely replied, "Uh, yeah. I'm happy."

Pastor Charles pressed in. "What are your thoughts when you're alone? Like, what were your thoughts today as you drove into Cedar Lake?"

John shoved his hands into his pockets and shifted his weight to the other foot. "Well, uh, just reminiscing about growing up," knowing he wasn't directly lying. A small bead of sweat broke out on his forehead and he slyly wiped it away, hoping Pastor Charles wouldn't notice. "Pastor Charles, I have great memories about this place and you. I learned a lot while I was here. As I told you, I'm still attending church in Chicago with my wife every Sunday and we volunteer a lot for many good causes."

The pastor reached out and put a hand on John's shoulder. "Do you know that you are forgiven, John?"

"I'm sorry, Pastor. Did I wrong you in some way?"

"No, John. Not me. Yourself. You've wronged yourself with insincere motives, the deep thoughts you attempt to hide with a very worthy exterior. God wants to make you whole, the inside matching the outside. It's deception, John, to cause someone to believe an untruth. But God knows you in your heart and He forgives you. This started back in high school and unless I'm wrong, it's continued all these years."

John felt for the back of the pew, steadying himself. "Are you sure you don't have me confused with my mischievous brother, Jake? He was always causing trouble for this town."

"John, your brother Jake doesn't deceive anyone. He is what he is, like it or not. What he feels on the inside, he acts on the outside, and all clearly see his feelings of resentment and disrespect. What I'm talking about started with you, in high school. It started with Selena Owens."

John collapsed into the pew.

Pastor Charles slid into the pew beside him. "It's okay, John. God forgives you. You've carried an unnecessary burden all these years and that has set up a pattern in your life. It's time to unravel what's been woven."

John blinked his watery eyes. "How did you know?"

"Selena came to me for prayer and advice. She was confused and didn't know what to do. I was her pastor, so I prayed. But, John, this is about you. I've been praying that you would be able to accept God's forgiveness some day and not continue to live with guilt. I need to tell you that you don't have to try so hard to get His forgiveness. You don't have to earn God's forgiveness. He's already given it to you. Just accept it." Pastor Charles paused. "John, imagine this. If you had a child," he said with tenderness in his eyes, "there would be nothing they could do that would cause you to not love them. Am I right?"

"Yes, I suppose you are."

"Believe me when I tell you that's how it is with God and His children." He patted John on the shoulder. "Now, if you will wait here for just a minute, I have something for you." Pastor Charles stood, walked down the aisle and left through the side door behind the communion curtain.

John stretched his legs and arms out, letting his head rest on the back of the pew. As he waited for Pastor Charles to return, he stared at the beam of light from the octagon window. Suddenly aware that some time had passed, he glanced at his watch: "4:23." He jumped to his feet and paced the aisle, eyeing the doorway where he anticipated Pastor Charles' return.

Pastor Charles came quickly running down the aisle, ready with an apology. "Sorry, Johnnie. Hope I am not making you late. I know you're in town to see Wilma. She phoned earlier today requesting prayer and said you were coming to visit." He handed John a sealed envelope with his name written on it. "This has been in my study for some time now. I think it's time to give it to you. Don't read it now. Get alone with God and read it."

With a quizzical expression, John accepted the envelope. "Sorry, Pastor Charles, but I do need to get going. A-Dub and Ray are expecting me at 4:30 and they won't like it if I am late. It was really good to see you and thank you for the lesson on God's forgiveness."

"John, it wasn't a lesson. It was a message from God that's been a long time coming."

John nodded his head and turned to exit the church. Stuffing the envelope into his coat pocket and giving it only a brief thought, he ran through the meditation garden to his car.

CHAPTER 5

John's tires squealed on the hot asphalt as he swung into Aunt Wilma and Uncle Ray's driveway five minutes late. They were sitting in their rocking chairs on the front porch, sipping iced tea.

John jumped out of the car and waved guilty hands in the air. "Sorry, sorry."

Wilma was shaking her head, "You're still drivin' like a teenager and you're still five minutes late."

"I've learned to drive aggressively in the city. You'll get run over otherwise." John bounded the two steps to the porch in one leap and threw his arms around Wilma in a bear hug. "Sorry about being late." Then he rustled Ray's hair and flopped down in the chair next to him.

"Want some tea?" asked Wilma.

"You know I do," said John, flashing a boyish grin. "Want me to get it?"

"No, I'm getting some more for myself and I gotta check on dinner." She disappeared into the house.

"How ya' been, Uncle Ray?"

"Keeping busy as usual. Once you get labeled as 'the Fix-it Man,' everybody comes around with a problem. I don't really mind though. Gives me something to do."

"How's the team looking this year?"

"Oh, they're not lookin' too bad. They're breaking in a new quarterback this year, so I don't think they'll beat the Wildcats. Never will be as good as when your brother was playing, though.

But you'll get to see for yourself at homecoming." He raised a questioning eyebrow at John.

Homecoming was a big event in Cedar Lake. The alums were honored at a dinner before the game, and many rode through the center of town on a Homecoming Parade float. If there were more honorees than could ride on the float, they walked. After the game, everyone in the town turned out for the carnival and street dance. John had not been to a homecoming game since high school, but had agreed to come this year because of Wilma's constant insistence.

"It's late September, isn't it?" John asked.

"Yep. Wilma says you and Treeny are staying here," said Uncle Ray with a smile and a twinkle in his eyes. "I'm looking forward to that." Uncle Ray stopped rocking as he added, "Jake is staying here, too. It's been a long time since we've all been together."

"You're right about that," said John, staring off into the clouds.

Wilma kicked the screen door open as she juggled two glasses of iced tea. "Let me help you with that," John said, as he hurried to take his glass of tea.

Settling back in their chairs, John asked, "So, where is it?"

"Right here," said Wilma as she reached inside the top of her bra. Her hand emerged with the lottery ticket between her thumb and forefinger, pinky raised in the air.

"A-Dub, I know you trust me, but I brought along some documents for you to sign. It's because you do trust me with this ticket that we have to make sure it's safe. Just in case anything would happen to me tonight or before I can get you a safety deposit box, I want you to sign a paper saying it belongs to you and you gave it to me for safekeeping."

She placed the ticket securely back inside her bra. "What are we gonna do, Johnnie?"

"We're gonna cash it in and invest it. That's my job. I take money and make more money from it."

"Johnnie, I don't even need this! What are we gonna do with *more* money?"

"The world always needs more money. There are lots of needs in this world and money can take care of them."

"I never thought we would win. We just played for fun. It gave us something to do and something to look forward to on Monday morning. We got all we need and all we want. Isn't that right, Ray?"

"Yep, Wilma." Ray turned to John. "Winnin' this throws a wrench into our plans. I guess Wilma told you we've signed up to live on The New World. Maybe we should just donate the money there, or sponsor some families who don't have the funds to go."

"Whoa, I didn't know you had already signed up to go. I thought you were still thinking about it. Are the girls going, too?" asked John, referring to Wilma's friends who played the lottery with her.

"Jean is the only one who hasn't decided. It's her heart. She's afraid the health care won't be good enough up there for the problems she has. They will only have clinics, and in her mind that means colds, flu, and stuff like that." Wilma walked to the edge of the porch and eyed her flower garden. "I figure the biggest worry I have is who's gonna take care of my beautiful yard."

"Hey, wait a minute," John chuckled. "You won't worry about me and Treeny?"

"No, Johnnie. You'll be just fine. I might worry about your brother, though. My biggest concern is that he's wasting his life. He's got so much to offer, if only he could get over his disappointments. I know God had a purpose for him after his injury, but he never got over feeling cheated. If he would ever realize that football was just a vehicle that God used to showcase his qualities, then he would get into another vehicle and keep driving."

John braced, silently waiting for this conversation to pass. Wilma read his body language and let her last sentence hang in the air.

After a few moments, Ray responded, "Don't know that there is much any of us can do that hasn't already been done."

"Amen to that," said John.

"Well, we better get inside and eat supper," said Wilma. "The girls will be here at 6:00. And . . . I haven't told them about the winnings. They know something's up, though. I was vague when I asked them to come over. I just said, 'Meet here tonight and don't tell anyone.'"

As they entered the house, John took in the familiar aroma of Wilma's cooking. This house, these people, this town were all very much a part of who he was today. He was thankful for the love and bonds he experienced while growing up. He sat down at the table and looked over at all the photographs of loved ones displayed on the buffet.

"Are you sure about going to The New World? I mean . . . have you really thought it all out?" he asked.

"Let's pray, John," said Ray, ignoring the question. He closed his eyes and bowed his head. "God, we are sooo thankful for all You have provided. We have had a good life, blessed with children we never thought we would have and friends who stand by us in every crisis of life. You have given us abilities and allowed us the opportunity to help others benefit by them. Now You have given us more. We believe You have allowed these winnings for a purpose. This has come to us and now we desire to know Your will in this matter." Ray interrupted his prayer and turned to his wife. "Wilma, let me see that ticket." She retrieved the ticket and laid it on the table. "Wilma, Johnnie, put your hand on the ticket." He laid his hand on top of theirs and continued to pray. "God, we dedicate these winnings to You. We don't desire wealth to be used for our own pleasures. We don't need a better place to live or more expensive cars to drive or fancier clothes to wear. We are more than satisfied with all that we have. But we believe this has come our way for a reason. We need Your wisdom in this. Please guide Johnnie. We trust You will give him Your direction for these winnings. Now, Lord, we thank You for the food we are about to eat. Amen."

Silently, they began to eat, each thoughtful about Ray's prayer. After a few minutes, John spoke. "We'll put all of this money in a trust fund until we reach a decision about what to do. That means, we cash in the ticket but hold it in an account, actually several accounts because of insurance limitation. I'll need to have the legal documents prepared first, and since it's a priority, I can have it expedited tomorrow. Can you come to Chicago tomorrow to sign the papers?"

"If we all take off work, it'll raise suspicion. I don't want anybody to know about this. Can you imagine the stir it will cause?"

"A-Dub, people are going to find out. Three of us know about it now. In about an hour, that number will double. And an hour after that, the number will double again. Everyone has someone he will tell. We just need the story to be something we want to be told. Money makes people go crazy. Everyone is going to want something from you. All the poor-me's and do-gooders will have their hands out. If this money is in a trust account, your answer to them will be easy. You won't have personal access to the money, and whatever you decide will be a group decision. Let's just hope the girls agree to this."

"Sounds like wisdom to me," said Ray as he began to clear the table of the supper dishes. "This way none of us are personally responsible for the money—it's too much of a decision for one person. We've relied on each other as friends over the years to help with our decisions, anyway. Why should this be different?"

"Let's hit this thing head on," said John. "Let me call the press and send a limo to pick you girls up tomorrow. Let everyone know. And celebrate this winning. You have a great opportunity to express your beliefs through this. You could even pick a couple of charities you want to donate to and we could announce that, too. We won't announce the amount you donate but don't give away too much. I just think it would be good press."

"I hadn't thought about it like that," said Wilma excitedly. "I was thinking like it was a curse and not a blessing. God's working fast after that prayer, Ray. I like this way of handling things. You're right, Johnnie. They're gonna know sooner or later anyway. Might as well jump in with both feet instead of tippy toein' around the edges." With that, Wilma scooted her chair back, got up and started dancing around the dining room. Her dance was infectious; Ray and John joined her, clapping and laughing.

Engrossed in their festivities, they didn't hear Margaret and Suzi come in earlier than planned. Standing in the double door opening between the living room and the dining room, Suzi asked, "Did we win or something? You been acting funny all day."

"Yep, we won alright," said Wilma, dancing over to Suzi and twirling around her. As she danced into the living room, Barbra Jean and Jean were pulling in the driveway. Out the door and onto the porch she danced, clapping and laughing. Suzi and Margaret looked at Ray and Johnnie with shrugs. The men followed Wilma out the front door with the girls in tow. Barbra Jean and Jean looked at each other and said in unison, "We must have won something this time!"

Barbra Jean called to Wilma, "How much did we win?"

"Shhh, not so loud. Let's all go into the house," ordered Wilma.

Once they were seated in the living room, they all calmed down. Johnnie spoke first, "I guess you all figured it out when you saw my car in the driveway. You did win the lottery. All of it. The news channels actually reported it a little on the low side. Instead of 750 million, the ticket is worth 798 million! The most in history!" John waited to hear a shout but no one spoke.

"Well . . . ? What do you think about that?" he asked.

Margaret solemnly spoke first, "That's a lot of money. A whole lot of money. What are we going to do with it?" As if that was their cue, they all began talking among themselves.

After several minutes of discussion, Wilma called the group to order, "Hey, listen everybody. Johnnie's got a solution. We need to listen to him."

"Girls, you don't need to decide tonight what you're going to do with the money. I am suggesting we form a trust for the entire amount. That means when you decide what to do with the money you will all need to agree, whether you split it equally among yourselves or whether you use all of it for one purpose. But this will protect you girls from being hit up by undeserving family and strangers. You have a lot to think over. I understand most of you are planning to live on The New World. I think the laws there may preclude you from taking this with you; I'll have to look into it. At any rate, let's claim the prize money and decide what to do with it later."

"That sounds like a smart idea, Johnnie," said Margaret.

"Yes," agreed Suzi.

Barbra Jean's response was, "I'm not prepared to make any other decision tonight besides that one."

Jean was the only reluctant one. "I'm not sure. I'm already the odd man out because I haven't decided to live on The New World. But, if you're saying we only need to do this trust fund thing tonight and decide about the money later, then I guess that makes sense. I don't know what else we would do tonight."

"A-Dub, let's go to your computer and open up a document I sent you this afternoon that we will all sign tonight agreeing to this. Then I'll take your lottery ticket to Indianapolis to claim your winnings. Let's set up your accounts first and get the official paperwork done, and then we'll announce it to the public."

"Ray, you and the girls get some of that apple pie I made yesterday," said Wilma, "and there's vanilla ice cream and caramel syrup, too." She and John went to her office to print the document.

Everyone chattered excitedly while Ray went to the living room and turned on the television. "Hey girls, come on! Let's get this special report on The New World started," he said as he settled into his comfy chair.

CHAPTER 6

Ray turned on the live television broadcast at 6:15. Wilma had suggested they record the special, but he continued to do things the old fashioned way, insisting the world didn't need to wait on him and that promptness was a virtue. America's sweetheart of a reporter, Shelly Katz, was interviewing Malachi Gentry, the Christian spokesman for The New World. Shelly was wrapping up a synopsis of the original three segments.

"Shhh, everybody get quiet! Let's listen to this," Margaret said. They gathered in the living room just as the commercial break ended. "Wilma! Johnnie! Get in here! The special on The New World started already." They quickly came into the living room and found seats. Ray gave up his comfy chair to bring in chairs from the kitchen for two of the girls. He and John stood beside the sofa.

"You stubborn old mule," said Wilma. "You were supposed to record this."

"Yeah, says you. We haven't missed anything. She just went over the first three specials which we already saw," said Ray.

Shelly's melodic, slightly southern accent immediately drew them in. "Welcome to the latest update on The New World. As you have just heard, the federal government and NASSA are pleased that the proposed occupation of this new nation has been well received by those of the Christian faith. Our first three reports were very popular. In fact, this network had its largest viewing audience during the last report," she bragged.

"It is apparent that Americans are interested in knowing the future of our country, our world, and our universe. And we should be. The times we live in are tenuous, but solutions are being sought on all fronts. The U.S. government and the National Administration of Scientific Space Advancement have teamed up with a winning proposal. Its success is imminent, a carefully-considered plan has been put into place for our exponentially growing population. As reported in the previous three specials, NASSA's New World will provide the solution for many of the problems we face now and in the future on this planet."

The camera panned a replica of The New World. Video streaming of the living quarters aired as she continued. "The first report was on the physical features of this man-made planet. Twenty-five years in the making, this New World is ready for occupation by humans. Climate-controlled pods will eliminate many of the weather challenges we face on earth, such as strong winds and extreme temperatures. Additional pods are proposed as the population increases. Each pod is seven square miles, designed as a planned community similar to those built in recent years in our country. Personal motorized transportation will not be necessary, as public transportation in the form of monorail and subway systems are an integral part of this new world. Food supplies will be fresh, grown in greenhouse environments. Vegetarianism will be encouraged as a cleaner way of eating. The slaughtering of animals will be illegal due to sanitation standards but meat supplies will come from earth in frozen form. Minimalism will be necessary, due to the allotment of 300 square feet of living space per individual." Shelly paused and took a deep breath. "It seems that NASSA has thought of everything."

The cameraman focused on Shelly again with a smiling photo of Dirk Deluca in the background. "The third report was our most compelling. I interviewed Dirk Deluca from Homeland Security about the impending disaster our country is facing if we do not find a way to disperse our population. Some of our landmasses collapsed several years ago due to the underground pockets created by the massive disaster with the great oil spill in the Gulf of Mexico. That disaster put an enormous stress on our natural resources and accelerated the search for alternative fuel sources. We also interviewed scientists who substantiated that we are using up our planet's resources as our population continues to increase. The world population doubled between the years of 1959 and 1999. We are currently facing another doubling of the population in only two-thirds that time. Mr. Deluca emphatically insists that we act now on this proposal where future growth can take place. The science and technologies exist, allowing this to happen, and Mr. Deluca explained the urgency of proceeding quickly with this proposal.

"Our second report, however, has been the most controversial, and will be the topic of discussion this evening. Malachi Gentry was featured in that report, whom some are calling a 'modern-day Moses.'" Shelly paused as the cameraman came in for a live close up of Malachi, looking uncomfortably into the camera. Shelly continued, "He has been appointed as an ambassador for this new Christian nation and has selected four chairpersons to help with the recruiting process. Christians are referring to The New World as 'The Kingdom of Heaven,' inferring that the life they seek will be structured around heavenly kingdom principles. The federal government has sponsored workshops for drafting the executive, legislative, and judicial systems. Educational standards have also been developed which will fill the needs of this New World. This has been a carefully thought-out plan by some of the world's greatest minds."

Shelly paused as she changed directions. "As explained in this previous report, the government has chosen to give this opportunity to people of the Christian faith. Some feel this is discriminatory, and tonight we will examine the reasons why the Christians have been chosen to participate in this initial exodus."

Shelly paused again, hoping the connection between "Moses" and "the exodus" would sink in. She had been strongly encouraged to help the public understand that Christians would be the best fit for this first initiative, so she methodically chose persuasive words.

"Let me introduce our discussion panel and give each panelist five minutes to respond to an opening question regarding this decision by our federal government at the recommendation of the National Disaster Relief Agency."

"Dirk Deluca is the Secretary of the Department of Homeland Security, previously the Administrator of the National Disaster Relief Agency. Congratulations to you, Mr. Deluca, on your new appointment. He has been instrumental in bringing this project together. While he was with NDRA, a new strategy emerged, one to avert impending disasters. NDRA clearly recognizes the biggest disaster Planet Earth is facing. This was the driving force behind their proposal. Thank you for joining us, Mr. Deluca." Shelly smiled as the cameraman drew in for a close up.

She continued, "Jodi Franks is the chief scientist and mastermind behind the physical construction of this fabricated planet. Her involvement began with the prototype 25 years ago in Bloomington, Indiana. Her real expertise, however, has come with designing the sanitation system, which will double as the mechanism for harvesting the fuel supply from the Earth's moon. Quite innovative, I understand. Tonight she will bring us a report on the studies of the physiological effects of living in this controlled environment and how that relates to the Christian segment of our population. Welcome, Ms. Franks."

Shelly faced the camera and spoke in a somber tone, giving serious attention to her next guest. "Malachi Gentry needs no introduction to most of our audience this evening. His face is familiar and his quotes are famous. His positive affirmation of every human being is contagious. He is outspoken about his Christian faith and believes The New World provides a welcome opportunity for anyone who desires to pursue this lifestyle without opposition." The cameraman opened the view of Shelly to include Malachi as she turned to face him. "Mr. Gentry, we will begin this discussion with the question on everyone's mind.

Can you tell us why this opportunity should be open only to those of the Christian faith?"

"First of all, let me say thank you, Shelly and this network, for allowing us the opportunity to explore these concerns. This is a unique situation, one that has never before been encountered. Technologies have exploded and the great minds at NASSA have built an option for our future. They have quietly put in place an answer to many of the problems the world currently faces. However, in the past, other men have also dreamed of perfect solutions for the dilemmas they faced. The variable is humanity, or the complex makeup of the human need. It comes natural for men to put themselves first, but the basic teaching of Christianity is to put others first. On The New World, these values will permeate the executive, judicial, legislative, and educational systems.

"The reason why Christians have been chosen by our government to live on The New World is that, in some respects, we are already a nation of like-minded people. We have our own culture and by-laws, and even though they are not written into law, we believe and live according to those age-old values. These principles and ideals are what every follower of Jesus Christ strives to live by. Christians gather regularly, at least once or twice a week, and learn Christian living. We have a code, called the Bible, which states our intentions and guides our actions.

"Another important point to consider is that Christianity is a choice. No one is coerced into believing or acting any certain way. I cannot state how important that is. People *choose* Christianity. We are not compelled by anyone to act a certain way. We choose. Therefore, the importance is this; we all act of our own free will. And as a Christian, our desire is to please God, not ourselves. That is the intention of everyone who calls himself or herself a Christian.

Normally, societies compel their citizens to act certain ways because someone thinks up a law for the best interest of their citizens. For example, take driving in America. We have a law that sets the speed limit. If you exceed that speed limit, you will get a ticket. We compel every citizen in America to obey the law of the speed limit. Someone decided that a certain speed would be dangerous if exceeded. Men of elected positions agreed and it became law. Then other laws were instituted to punish those who exceed the speed limit. And still other laws were instituted to punish those who exceed the speed limit excessively." He paused and took a deep breath. "My point is, you can continue to regulate behavior, but the heart of a person remains unchanged. No doubt the person receiving the ticket will continue to exceed the speed limit while driving. The Christian population is concerned with the heart, because when the heart of a person is changed, the behavior will also change. They will desire to comply with laws to please God; they won't need to be compelled by laws or societies to act with respect for others. They will respect others, because they have become a spiritual people whose behavior is in harmony with God."

Shelly broke in to clarify his rhetoric. "So, are you saying that you won't need laws? That everyone will act responsibly because he wants to? You don't think that's a bit naïve?"

"No, Shelly. That's not what I'm saying. If that were true, then the original Christians wouldn't have needed the Ten Commandments that God gave to Moses. My case for the Christians is due to morals and values that exist because of conformity to Biblical standards which have been around for a couple of thousand years. Other segments of our society would need to spend more time developing their culture, while the Christian culture already exists. I'm saying I believe Christians are more prepared to live on The New World."

"What about other religious groups in our country? Why not give them the opportunity instead of Christians?" Shelly asked the other question that was on everyone's mind.

"There are more Christians in this country than any other religion. I understand from Mr. Deluca that is the reason we have been selected."

"Thank you, Mr. Gentry, for your comments."

Shelly, abruptly changing the direction of the conversation, questioned Dirk next. "Mr. Deluca, could you dispel concerns about Christians and their voting habits? It's been rumored that those in government would like to do away with the third party that gets the majority of Christian votes. They say we would have better qualified politicians if we returned to the two political parties of years past. They contend that the 'Moral Majority' vote goes to that third party and hinders progress by splitting the country in too many directions."

Deluca shifted in his chair and cleared his throat as he answered. "It's a known fact that Christians have banded together to vote on moral issues according to their Biblical standards. However, dispersion seems to be taking place naturally. We are finding that many Christians are compromising those strict standards due to societal trends. The People's Poll has shown this to be true. I believe if we wait much longer, the Christians may not necessarily be the right choice. They would need to undergo as much training to live together as any other segment in our society." Dirk smiled as he worked a sense of urgency for Christians into his answer.

"Thank you, Mr. Deluca. We will return right after this announcement." Shelly winked at Dirk as the network aired a commercial from their sponsor.

"That's for sure," Ray said loudly. "We gotta get outta here before there's no more Christians. We're starting to act just like everybody else." The girls all chimed in at the same time, chattering about their opinions, sounding like a gaggle of geese heading south for the winter.

CHAPTER 7

"**S**hh, girls! I gotta answer the phone," shouted Ray over the chatter.

"Hell . . . ooo."

Wilma saw Ray grimace, straighten his back, and stare out the front window.

"How bad is it?" Ray asked the caller as he pushed open the screen door and walked out on the porch. The girls shrugged and continued to watch the Special Report. Wilma followed Ray outside.

A deep voice with a southern accent slowly answered Ray's question. "It's real bad, Mr. Smith. This time, it's real bad. He's in the hospital at Chinle, which ain't the best place for medical care, but it was the closest place we could take him. He got in a fight last night and he's been in a coma."

Ray had never met Jimmy McDowell, but he liked the sound of his calm, controlled voice. Most of all, though, Ray liked Jimmy's concern for Jake. Jake had described him as six foot tall, a barrel chested, red-faced, redheaded, hairy Irishman with a temperament quite the opposite of his intimidating physique. During their few conversations over the years about Jake's skirmishes, Ray had discovered a handful of other details about Jimmy, including that he had moved to the Navajo Indian reservation in Arizona from West Virginia. As a teenager, he had gone on two mission trips to the reservation to help with children's Bible school. As an adult, he moved onto the reservation and attempted to make a difference in the lives of the people for whom he had developed strong compassion.

"Should we come?" asked Ray.

"The doctor said he didn't think there was much hope. He said we just gotta wait it out. And, well, there's the little girl. She needs somebody to look after her. I don't think Gravél can do it proper." He hesitated a moment, "You know 'bout her, don't ya'?"

"Yes, but Jake just told us about her recently. He was gonna bring her to meet us in a couple of months." Ray kicked at a maple seed on the porch. "He was planning a visit with us."

"She sure is sweet. My wife and I could take her for a little while, but with our five kids—well, we think she would be better off with family. We hope you understand. Besides that, we're afraid she'll get too attached to us. She's been through a lot, you know."

"Sure we do. We can't thank you enough for looking after her and for looking after Jake. Have you seen him . . . I mean, what's your opinion? Do you agree with the doctor?"

"I don't know, Mr. Smith. He took a lotta hard blows to the face but that kick to his head, well, it took him down. That son of a gun he fought was mean. I tried to talk Jake out of fightin' him, but he's got a lot of anger. He was hell-bent on this fight. I went by yesterday afternoon to try to talk some sense into him, but I couldn't persuade him."

"So, this fight was planned? He wasn't jumped?" Ray asked, surprised by the possibility.

"There's a lot of bored people on the reservation, so Jake set up a fight club in back of The Gulch. They rotated the night of the fights to avoid the law and this time it was on Sunday. Jake never fought before but somebody challenged him. That was all it took. You know, he's bullheaded and likes to be 'The Man.' I think the guy he fought was on 'roids or sump'n. He was meaner'n anybody I ever seen. Everybody knew 'bout Jake's head, you know, the blood clot thing. This guy looked like he was tryin' to *kill* Jake. There was blood spurting all over the place.

Jake couldn't get a punch in. What got him was that kick to the side of the head. Then he went down . . . *hard*. It was bad." Jimmy's voice started to crack.

"Thanks for all you're doing, Jimmy. We'll get on the first flight we can." Ray reached for the scratch pad and pencil he kept in his shirt pocket. "Now give me your phone number and directions to the hospital."

Ray hung up the phone and turned to Wilma. Shaking his head, he said, "Why in the world would he risk his life? Jake knew what one more blow to his head might mean."

"What's happened, Ray?" Wilma wanted more facts than Ray was willing to deliver at the time, as he pondered the call.

"What makes Jake tick? He's been blessed in life with skills and opportunity, but he's turned all of his advantages inward. If he would only see how he could make a positive difference if he used what God has given him to benefit others. He just can't see beyond his own needs or disappointments."

Wilma put her hand on Ray's arm. "He's gonna be alright, Ray. I have faith that someday, somehow, he will be able to turn his life around."

"Now he's got that little girl. That should make him want to live differently." He stood quietly staring at the sky.

"Wilma, I gotta go to my praying place," he said as grabbed the corner post to steady himself and jumped off the end of the porch. He left the details of the conversation a mystery to Wilma. He knew she would understand and allow him this time. In an emergency, he always processed things with God first, and Wilma was accustomed to this behavior. When Ray emerged from spending time with God, he would have assurance that God would lead him. In times like this, Ray was glad Wilma had her friends. She and the girls liked to kick things around among themselves first and then ask God.

Behind the stack of firewood in his workshop, Ray had set up a camp cot with a side table, a lamp, and a Bible. This is where he talked to God; then he listened and God talked to him.

"God, Jake's got himself into a big mess now. But, maybe, just maybe, this will be his time. We've prayed so hard over the years that he could turn his life around, and even though this looks bad, maybe it had to get this bad for him to make a change. I'm not givin' up on him and I know You won't either. You love him more'n we do. I know You're gonna help him pull out of this. I can't even think the outcome would be any different than him turning his life around. Please God, *please God*, give him another chance. He will be great for You. I know it and have always known it. He's got greatness in him. He's just been fighting with himself all these years. Let the Jake You made emerge this time . . ." Ray continued for some time until he saw John standing beside him.

"Uncle Ray, please come in and tell us what's going on. A-Dub is beside herself since she only heard half a conversation. Is Jake alright?"

"I don't know, Johnnie. That's what I been prayin' about. Let's go back in and I'll tell all of you what I do know."

The special on The New World had ended and everyone was waiting for Ray in the kitchen. "Who called, Ray?" asked Wilma.

"That was Jimmy McDowell. You know, he's the guy that Jake has known over the years—his rescuer—well, more like a guardian angel, I think. Anyway, Jake's really in trouble this time," said Ray as he slumped down in a chair and buried his head in his hands.

"What is it, Ray?" Wilma asked.

"Jake got into a fight and he's in a coma."

"A fight!?" blurted John. "What happened?"

"Yeah, seems like they have some kind of fight club in back of his store. A guy challenged Jake and the bullheaded son of a gun took him up on it. Landed him in the hospital. It's serious, this time. They don't know if he's gonna make it."

Wilma dropped her shoulders and walked out the back door. John followed her. "A-Dub, it's going to be okay."

"I don't know, Johnnie. God keeps giving him chances to change his ways. This time, he might have gone too far. You know there's a little girl. I thought having her might help him want to live a better life."

"Little girl? I don't know about a little girl."

Wilma turned to John. Tears filled her eyes. "Jake's got a little girl. I think she's four. She's been living with Jake about six months now."

"Where's her mother?"

"She died because of a drug overdose. She was living with a friend, but she had a will that left custody of the girl to Jake, who she said is the father. Jake had it confirmed with a paternity test. So he's had custody."

"Why didn't I know about this?"

"I was hopin' to tell you tonight but you asked me not to talk about him. Anyway, the time just hasn't been right. Jake was bringing her with him homecoming week so we could all meet her."

"How can he manage having a child living with him? He can't even manage his own life."

"He hired a nanny to watch her at the store while he took care of business. He said he fixed a playroom for her. On nights he doesn't make it back to pick her up, the nanny's daughter comes to spend the night at the store and looks after her. I think everybody who knows Jake knows about his problems, and he flashes money in their faces so he can get about anything done. But we got other things to be concerned about right now. We need to go to Jake. I'm going to check on flights." She turned and walked back into the house, where the girls had circled around Ray and were consoling him.

"Ray, we need to get on the first flight out. The closest airport is in Albuquerque and then we can rent a car. I don't think we can make it to Jake before tomorrow night. I'm going to the computer to see what flight I can get tomorrow morning."

Ray stood and spoke with authority as if to convince himself as well as the others. "Jake is going to be okay. This is the time God's been waiting for. He's going to turn it around. I just know it. Let's go to him as soon as we can, Wilma."

Margaret spoke, "John, we're going to need to put this lottery thing on hold 'til we figure out what's going on with Jake."

"Well, girls, this document we drew up puts the money in a safe place for now. All you need to do tonight is sign it and I'll take care of the rest. You do trust me, don't you?" John asked flashing his boyish grin and trying to lighten the mood.

"Gimme that pen," said Suzi. "I'm kind of glad we don't have to make a quick decision. There's a lot to think about."

Each lady took her turn signing the document and Ray signed as a witness. Wilma returned with news about flights, but they encouraged her to sign the document first so they could put that matter to rest. As the girls began to leave, John's phone sent him a message from Treeny. He stuffed the papers into his briefcase and answered her message. "B hm 1 hour."

"What did you find out about flights tomorrow, A-Dub?" John asked.

"Kinda early: eight-thirty. But if we don't do it then, we'll have to wait until four o'clock. That would mean we wouldn't get to see Jake 'til Wednesday." She turned to Ray with a question in her eyes.

"Looks like we get up early," he shrugged.

"What about the security clearance we need? Do you know how we can get that, Johnnie?" asked Wilma.

"If you check in two hours early, you can fill out the computerized forms they provide at the terminals. Otherwise, you wouldn't get clearance for twenty-four hours," John advised.

"That means we will need to get a real early start in the morning," said Wilma.

"I could meet you at the airport," said John. "I am familiar with how things work and it could help speed you along."

"That would be great, Johnnie," said Ray.

"We better say goodnight if we're going to get any sleep," said Wilma.

Johnnie kissed A-Dub on the cheek. Ray walked him to the car. Johnnie gave him a squeeze around the shoulder. "It's going to be all right."

"Yep. I think you're right, Johnnie."

John left the Cedar Lake town limits and pulled onto 135th Street. He activated the voice command to Treeny. "Hi, babe. Sorry I'm so late. We had a lot to talk about and the girls came over, too. We got a call about Jake and it's not good." He began to fill her in on the details and as he drove past Charlie Trotter's farm, he didn't even notice it.

CHAPTER 8

Louie Gravél ranted in his thick French accent while stuffing clothes into a suitcase. "That should fix him for good! I'm tired of cleaning up his messes and living like this. I don't want to be a babysitter no more, not to him or that kid. I've cleaned up his puke for the last time. No more!" His long gray hair was braided in a single braid mid-way down his back. Traditional turquoise jewelry on both hands and wrists implied he had bought into the culture on the reservation where such things implied a certain status.

A loud banging on the door interrupted his grumblings.

"What do you want?" shouted Gravél.

"You know what I want. My money!"

Gravél swore under his breath, "I'm coming." He opened the door as far as the chain lock would permit and peered out. He held out his fist, clenched around a roll of bills, to the man on the other side, a muscular Navajo. Gravél had hoped to satisfy him quickly but the man, dressed in a tired blue jean shirt with wisps of gray scattered in his almost black hair became insistent.

"That don't look like enough."

"That's it, that's all I got for you."

"That's bull," he shouted as he kicked the door hard enough to rip the chain lock out of the wood, overpowering Gravél's blockade. Towering over Gravél, he grabbed his hand, shaking it until the wad of money fell to the floor. "You weasel, you better not cheat me! It better all be here!" He tore off the rubber band

and started counting the money. Noticing the suitcase on the sofa, he asked, "You goin' somewhere?"

"Yeah, I'm taking a vacation. What's it to you, anyway?"

He glanced at Gravél as he continued to count the money. "You're short, Gravél! By twenty thousand bucks! I ought to kick your head in like I did that guy tonight. But since I'm a decent guy, I'm gonna give you a chance to pay up."

"That fight didn't pull in as much as I planned on, Vic. I'm going to need some time to come up with the rest."

"That's a lie! I know good and well the bets were on him. The odds were great for us to come up big winners, just like you said. I heard somebody say it was fifty to one. According to that, you made 250 thousand g's and I want mine! I did what you paid me to do; now I want what's coming to me! Maybe a little more for my troubles! Vic shoved Gravél up against the wall, fist up to his face. "So pay up now, Gravél!"

Sweat beaded on Gravél's forehead. "I'm telling you, we gotta get out of here fast! Jake's in the hospital in Chinle. One of my boys followed the guy that took him there and he says Jake's in a coma. If he doesn't make it, there's gonna be an investigation and I don't want to be around for that." Gravél loosened himself as Vic's grip relaxed and pushed past him to finish shoving his clothes in the suitcase. He grabbed a black duffle bag from the corner. "Come on. I'll give you the rest when we get to Flagstaff."

"Flagstaff? What's in Flagstaff?"

"Money, stupid."

"Don't you have it with you here? Where's the rest of the cash from tonight?"

"Listen, there are things you don't know. You'll have to trust me if you want your money."

"You kiddin' me? Trust you? You were about to leave without giving me anything."

"Then stay here. It's okay with me."

"Alright, but I'm not letting you out of my sight."

As they walked out into the gravel parking lot, Gravél noticed the only other vehicle in the lot was Jake's truck. "Where's your car?"

"Think I'm *stupid* or something? I don't want nobody to know I'm here."

As Gravél threw the duffle and suitcase in the back seat of his truck, he heard an odd sound in the distance. He stopped and turned around, scanning the perimeter. By the light of the full moon, he could see a small child sitting on a large rock, out by the fencerow.

"What is that?" grunted Vic.

"That's Jake's kid," he said to Vic. "I don't have time for this" Gravél cursed under his breath as he approached her. "You need to get inside *now*."

"But I didn't have supper and I'm hungry," came the sniffled reply.

"Where's the nanny?" Gravél snapped.

"I don't know. I'm hungry," and she cried louder.

"Get inside and stop your cryin'! Go to bed. Then you won't be hungry."

The barefoot little girl rubbed her eyes as she walked toward the playroom, making a wide berth around Vic. She looked up at him as she passed, her big brown eyes pooled with tears.

"What's the matter with you?" shouted Vic to Gravél, who was following the child. "She's just a kid. Can't you take a minute to give her something to eat?"

Gravél swore loudly. "Oh, all right!" He remotely locked the truck with the key fob, implying that Vic had better not get any ideas. Grabbing the little girl by the arm, he marched her into the playroom Jake had built onto the shop. In the kitchen, he rummaged around until he found some bread and peanut butter. He impatiently slapped together a sandwich and thrust it at her. "Now eat that and go to bed."

While Gravél was gone, Vic slipped a phone from his shirt pocket and punched in a number. He said softly, "Yeah, it's me. You had it pegged. We're leaving for Flagstaff right now."

Quickly stuffing the phone back into his pocket, he retrieved a pack of cigarettes. He pulled a lighter from his pants pocket, lit up, took a long drag, and paced the length of the truck until Gravél returned.

Gravél locked the deadbolt on the playroom door as he left.

"You gonna leave her in there alone?" questioned Vic.

"She's all right. The nanny will be here in the morning."

"Did you give her something to eat?"

"Aw, shut up. You probably killed her father tonight and you're worried about her being hungry?"

Vic stamped out his cigarette and got in the passenger side of the truck. Gravél jammed the keys into the ignition and they sped away in a cloud of dust.

*   *   *

Jimmy McDowell arrived at The Gulch around 5:00 a.m. He had been up all night, and the ER doctor assured him there was nothing he could do at the hospital. They would keep Jake under observation for the next 24 hours. Jimmy had walked the halls of the Chinle hospital, praying until about 4:00 a.m. Jake was a friend, but not in the traditional sense. Jimmy had put all of the effort into this relationship; Jake had contributed nothing. Suddenly, Jimmy got an urge to drive to Gravely's Gulch to check on things. During the forty-five minute drive, he had time to think about his relationship with Jake.

He recalled the times he stopped by the Gulch to check in on Jake to make sure he was all right. Many times he had found Jake slumped over a bar stool, nearly passed out, while Gravél was playing on-line poker in the back office. The place would be filthy and Jimmy would straighten things up before he took Jake home. Other times, he would pass Jake's truck in the ditch, with Jake "sleeping it off" in the front seat. Jimmy would sober him up, pull his truck out of the ditch, and follow him home.

Jake was Jimmy's personal project. He had vowed to God that he would never give up on Jake. Tonight, however, that vow was challenged. Jimmy was weary of his burden and this incident tonight was all he could take. He argued to himself that Jake was too stubborn even for God. He poured out his heart to God as the early morning air whistled through the open windows of his truck and drowned out his words.

"God, I know the Bible tells us that You will never put more on us than we can bear, but I am getting weary of this man You've asked me to befriend. He is bent toward destroying himself and all of his relationships. I question how many more times he can escape death. He doesn't seem to want to live or he wouldn't keep this up. Sometimes I don't think I can keep this up. It feels like I'm putting a bandage on a ruptured artery. This fight tonight . . . these brain injuries . . . his daughter . . . Gravél and all his sleazy friends . . . bootlegging . . . payoffs. He's not a good influence on anyone and I don't see any glimmer of hope for him. He never acknowledges You in any way. He mocks You, but I know You love him. You must see some purpose 'cause I still feel You prompting me to see after him. So here I am again, praying for his life. Let him live, please. Most of all, let him be of some good to others. Heal his hurts. Forgive him Lord, 'cause he doesn't know what he's doing. And Lord, please give me the strength to keep this up."

Jimmy's burden felt a little lighter as he pulled into the parking lot of The Gulch. Everything was quiet. No cars were in the lot and no lights were on inside. He pulled around back, and the only vehicle he saw was Jake's Tundra. He wondered why he didn't see Gravél's Silverado or at least the nanny's rusted green pickup. He parked and quietly got out. The security light was dimly illuminating the entrance to the playroom and he could see the doorway to Gravél's apartment behind the store. Jimmy, looking in every direction and listening intently, approached the apartment door and knocked lightly, fully aware of Gravél's temperament. He waited then knocked again, a little louder this time. Still no answer. He pulled out his phone, gave a command, and Gravél's number started to ring. Voice mail.

Jimmy approached the door to the playroom. He remembered Jake had given him a key for this door and he went back to his truck to search for it in the glove compartment. He retrieved a key buried under an assortment of packaged condiments and napkins. He tapped lightly on the door before he tried the key. It was the right one. He slowly pushed the door open and called softly for the nanny. He said her name a little louder as he stepped into the room . . . and nearly tripped over something on the floor.

"Ohhh, you hurt me," said a sad, weepy voice from the heap. Jimmy jumped back and fumbled for the light switch.

"Oh, baby, I'm sorry. What are you doing sleeping on the floor?" He reached down and scooped up the little girl with her teddy bear and blanket.

"I'm afraid. That mean man locked me in here. I was trying to run away but he made me come back."

"Where's nanny?" Jake asked her.

"I don't know. She didn't come today. But a whole bunch of trucks with lots of men came." She began to cry, "I want to see my mommy. I don't like it here."

Jimmy sat down with her in his lap in a nearby rocking chair. "Your mama can't come, honey. You know that. But I think you better come and stay at my house for a while."

She looked up at him with her chocolate-drop eyes. "You mean it, Mr. Jimmy? I can come to your house? I like it there."

"Your Granny A-Dub and Pawpaw Ray are coming to see you. They're coming all the way from Indiana."

"I don't 'member them."

"They're your daddy's mom and dad. Your daddy got hurt tonight and they're coming to see him. But everything's gonna be okay. I promise." Jimmy hugged Christina a little closer. "We better pack a bag for you and get going." Christina jumped down from his lap and ran into a back sleeping room to get her bag. Jimmy followed.

"Mr. Jimmy, I better get everything. I don't think I'm comin' back. I been praying and I saw an angel wearing a pretty blue dress. When I closed my eyes, I was wearing her pretty blue dress at a party with mommy and daddy."

"So you pray?" asked Jimmy.

"Oh, yeah, Mr. Jimmy. You taught me how."

"That's good, Christina, 'cause God cares about us even if it looks like nobody else does." He helped her with her bag as they left the playroom.

*　*　*

"Man, you better slow down a little," shouted Vic. "You know the cops look for any excuse to search us."

"Shut up. I'll drive any way I want to," hollered Gravél.

Gravél scanned for potential traps as the full moon lit up the desolate landscape. His mind drifted to his first encounter with the Navajo Nation police, reminding him that they had their own form of law, like an old wild-west movie. One evening after hours, the police came to check on things. He was accosted, bullied, and stuffed into the closet overnight, only to find the next day that the premium bottles of liquor in his private stash were missing. So was all the money from the register. From that time on, Gravél treated them very generously.

Gravél flew over the wavy roads, causing Vic to buck like a rodeo bull in his seat. Gravél swore at no one in particular as he voiced his opinion about the politics in Navajo Nation. "Those stingy politicians would rather spend that federal money on new trucks instead of take care of these roads. I'm sure it pained them to pave even one third of the of roads here. And a lousy paving job at that." Vic didn't respond; he just continued bumping up and down.

Gravél couldn't get to Flagstaff fast enough, but he needed to come up with a way to ditch Vic. If only he had escaped a few minutes sooner, he wouldn't have to deal with this now. A .22 between the eyes would be the quickest way to get rid of Vic, but that was too risky. He knew a distinguished Frenchman wouldn't survive the bullies in prison. Overpowering a man of

Vic's strength and size was out of the question. The trick would be to escape from his sight with all the money.

"I'm telling you, slow down!" hollered Vic. "You've been driving this reservation road long enough to know what's up ahead."

Gravél was well aware of the sharp curve at the top of the very steep hill they were climbing. The rocky terrain prevented seeing the curve until one was right upon it. The yellow warning sign had rusted and barely noticeable as it blended with the color of the earth. Off to the right, about three quarters of the way up the hill, was a dirt road leading to a party spot used by the young people. As Gravél's momentum increased, defying Vic's order, a police car pulled out from behind a large rock formation, lights flashing and siren screaming as it took up pursuit of the speeding truck.

"Look what you done now," shouted Vic.

Gravél swore. "We can fix this pretty quick." He ordered Vic, "Grab a hundred bucks outta that duffle." He slowed down and pulled the truck to the side of the road just before the curve.

Vic struggled to turn his large frame around in the front seat of the truck, clumsily groping for the duffle bag. He located it, grabbed it firmly, and hoisted it into the front seat as Gravél came to a halt on the shoulder of the road. Vic ripped the zipper open and gasped at the amount of money he saw in the bag. "You lying son of a @#*&. There's more money in here . . ."

"Shut up and hide that bag," Gravél interrupted. "I don't want these guys getting greedy. Gimme that hundred . . . and keep your hands off the rest of it."

Vic complied but added, "Thought the rest was in Flagstaff." He continued to hold the bag in his lap as the police officer, his hand on his revolver, approached Gravél's side of the truck.

"Outta the car, nice and slow," ordered the officer. "And put your hands up where I can see 'em."

Gravél grabbed the $100 bill before he slid out of the truck. "Sorry, officer. I know I was traveling fast. Just in a hurry to make a flight in Flagstaff," he lied. He held both hands in the air, with the bill between his thumb and forefinger.

"On the ground, face down. You, too," he shouted at Vic. "Get out of the truck."

Vic slid the duffle bag onto the floor and eased out of the truck. He came around the back of the truck with his hands slightly raised to his shoulders. As he approached, he saw the officer bending down, holding his drawn weapon against Gravél's head while his heavy boot rested on Gravél's back.

"What's the problem, officer?" Gravél wanted to know. "I was only speeding."

"Well, the problem is, my boss doesn't like you." Coldly, the officer squeezed the trigger, firing a shot directly in the back of Gravél's head.

Vic had come around the back of the truck just in time to witness Gravél take his last breath. "#@*&, man! I didn't know you were gonna do that! You were only supposed to knock him out." He stared at Gravél's lifeless body. "Is he dead?"

"He better be. That's what my orders were. Now help me get this body back into the truck." The officer plucked the bill from Gravél's hand and stuffed it in his pants pocket.

Vic's hands were shaking as he stooped to lift Gravél's body. "This is more than I signed up for. Murder wasn't a part of the deal. An accident is one thing, but cold-blooded murder is an entirely different matter."

The officer stared at Vic. "Want some of the same thing?" he asked, leveling the revolver at Vic's temple. Vic shook his head and the officer holstered his weapon. Vic continued helping the officer lift Gravél from the dirt. They each took an arm and attempted to stand Gravél upright. The body was limp, and slid back into the dirt, face up. Vic jumped back, horrified at the wretched expression on Gravél's face.

"Sissy," said the officer. "Grab his arm and let's get this done."

They wrestled with the body until they propped it up behind the steering wheel. As soon as Vic closed the door, he wiped the blood and dirt from his hands onto his shirt and pants. He choked back the vomit.

"Now, that makes you an accessory to murder," the officer said before walking back to the squad car. Opening the trunk, he began changing out of his bloody clothes.

Vic stood frozen, unable to think or move until a commanding voice, in a strong Navajo accent, pierced the silence. "Get the money and bring it over here." Vic recognized the familiar voice from the squad car. He walked to the passenger side of Gravél's truck, glancing at the dead body slumped over the steering wheel. Mechanically, he retrieved the duffle bag full of money.

"Is there another bag?" shouted the voice from inside the police car.

"A suitcase," hollered Vic.

"See if there's any money in it and bring it, too."

Vic located the suitcase in the truck bed and opened it. He found money among the clothes. Vic shakily sorted through Gravél's belongings and separated out the money, stuffing it in his own jacket since there was no room in the duffle bag. He stumbled back to the squad car. Opening the back door, he heaved the duffle bag onto the seat.

"Put the rest of it in that bag," commanded the passenger in the police car.

Vic unloaded his jacket of the money and placed it into the grocery sack he found on the back seat. Then he got in.

Keeping his back to Vic, the passenger lit a cigarette. Taking a drag, he calmly said to the officer standing outside the car, "Now let's finish this." The officer walked back to Gravél's truck and threw his own bloody clothes in the truck bed. He returned to the squad car, getting in behind the wheel, slid the key into the ignition, and put the car in reverse. He eased backward onto the dirt road leading to the party spot. After a short distance, they stopped where a wrecker had been parked behind a huge boulder.

"Think you can handle the rest of this?" the passenger asked Vic.

"Yeah, if you mean the accident we planned."

"That's what I mean."

"What about my money?" Vic wanted to know.

"Finish this and then we'll divide it up. Tomorrow night. We'll meet at Hoot 'n' Holler's in Flagstaff, just like we planned, only tomorrow, not tonight."

Vic looked down at his bloody clothes and stammered. "Just for the record, Norm, I don't like the way you changed things tonight. Taking a man's money is one thing, but taking his life, well . . . that's another thing altogether. He would have been broke but he would have survived the wreck."

"Oh, shut up," Norm said. "You'll have enough to soothe your conscience. Oh, one more thing, since you're so fond of changes," he added, "torch the vehicle before you push it off the cliff. We don't want any remaining evidence of that gunshot. There's a can of gasoline and some old rags in the wrecker."

Vic got out of the police car and slowly walked to the wrecker where the keys were in the ignition; he located the gas can and rags on the floor of the truck cab. He put the truck in gear and the police car followed him as he pulled around the boulder and down the dirt road. When they hit the pavement, Vic turned to go up the hill and the police car turned the opposite way. Vic noticed their brake lights in his rear view mirror. He dutifully followed through with torching and wrecking Gravél's truck by pushing it off the cliff at just the right spot in the curve. The police officer and his passenger drove away once they were satisfied that Vic had done the job right. Vic turned the wrecker around and followed them at a distance for a while before turning off onto a dirt road that led to his home. Once the lights from the police car faded from sight, Vic stopped the wrecker and got out. He paced around, sobbing, wringing his hands and ripping at the bloodied clothes.

CHAPTER 9

John's sleepless night turned too quickly into an early morning at the Midway airport. Mentally guarding the winning lottery ticket had taken priority over sleep. Seven hundred ninety eight million dollars was a lot to consider, and he couldn't wait to get to the bank where the ticket would be safe. But the banks weren't open yet, and he first had to meet A-Dub and Uncle Ray at the airport. John expected the comprehensive airport security inspections might upset them, since they were unaccustomed to flying. They would require the full two hours before flight time. Security measures were tighter than ever due to an increase in rogue acts of violence over the previous ten years. These delays had become the new norm for air travelers.

John was waiting when his aunt and uncle arrived at the airport. After they checked in, A-Dub asked him where he was carrying the ticket so he discreetly unbuttoned his shirt to show her a plastic baggie taped to his body, just left of his belly button.

"Good idea," she said quietly, "can't lose it there."

John's next order of business after seeing A-Dub and Ray off was to stop at the bank and put the lottery ticket in a safe deposit box, along with the paperwork the girls had signed the night before.

Alone in the secure room, he ripped off the medical adhesive tape and the baggie. It stung a little, but he was relieved when the lottery ticket was safely in the box. Even though it was only 11 o'clock, he was beginning to feel the effects of his sleepless night. He stopped at his favorite coffee shop for a double shot of espresso before going to the office.

Settling behind his desk, he turned on his computer and began researching investment options. A call on his private phone interrupted him before he had the chance to begin planning. It was Treeny.

"How's my Treeny girl?"

"Hey, babe. Missed my morning kiss."

"Yeah, sorry. I had to get to the airport early with A-Dub and Uncle Ray. They were clueless about airport security."

"Any news about Jake this morning?"

"No, nothing yet."

"We still on for dinner at Cozy's?"

"Err. It's going to be hard to do. I'm just getting my day started and there's a ton to do. With the news of Jake, I didn't get a chance to tell you I got a new client yesterday. This one is going to take all of my time for a little while." He leaned back in his chair and smiled.

"Pretty demanding, huh?"

"You have no idea. But on the upside, if all goes well, it could set us up for life."

Treeny was silent.

"This one is a sure thing, Treeny. I mean, I could retire from this rat race. Just a couple more years . . . or less."

The silence continued.

"Treeny, really. This one is for sure. Trust me."

"Okay, so when *will* I see you?" She tapped her foot as she stared at the scraps of fabric and drawings strewn around her workroom.

"I don't know, but it will be late. Don't wait up—and thanks for understanding. I'll make it up to you, I promise."

John hung up the phone. He desperately wanted to tell her about A-Dub's winnings, but now was not the time, not over the phone. They needed a night out and Cozy's would have been the perfect setting, but in light of these pressing circumstances, it would have to wait and she would have to forgive him.

His assistant knocked on his door.

"Come in."

"Mr. Minda, here are the portfolios of the clients that you asked for."

John was in the habit of seeing the hardcopy of important information. He preferred something tangible; something to hold in his hand for the assurance it wouldn't be compromised through the Internet. A superbug two years ago had made him jumpy. His top five clients had their on-line information stolen, but his firm had survived an investigation by the Federal Trade Commission and a news media exposé. He salvaged most of his clients—but not all of them—despite the FTC finding his firm blameless. The firm installed new security measures, but John made it a practice from then on to hardcopy important information. He also made it a practice to have delicate documents hand couriered, both ways.

John's assistant politely laid the folders on the edge of his desk and before she turned to leave she asked, "Is there anything else, Mr. Minda?"

"Uh, yeah. Could you call Flowers for All Occasions and have something colorful—er, something in blue if that exists in flowers—sent to Treeny at the shop? Add a note, 'Please forgive me. I'll make it up to you.'"

"Sure thing, Mr. Minda."

"Make sure they send it this afternoon, will you?"

The portfolios that lay before him were Wilma and Ray's, and two of the four friends who shared in the lottery win, Margaret and Barbra Jean. All had prospered nicely due to John's abilities to play it safe and be risky at the same time. Suzi and Jean needed help with planning their financial future, but their personal circumstances made them shortsighted about such matters. After the funeral of Suzi's husband and her son, she couldn't think about investments. Emotionally, she could barely survive each day, having lost both in a car accident. Jean had suffered from recurring health issues that drained all her resources; her income from Corny's only covered living expenses. Wilma and Ray's investments generated dividends they all but ignored. They loved giving to others and helping when they could, but as far as they were concerned, they didn't have any needs that weren't already met. Margaret and Barbra Jean made conservative investments that would allow them to live comfortably well into their future with some left over as an inheritance for their children.

John flipped through the three portfolios, considering what changes he might recommend. Everything was diversified and solid. That is, when they all had planned to retire in Cedar Lake. Now things would change since they decided to live on The New World. The New World's financial system was not based on capitalism, and promised a society structured on the care and concern of its citizens. Money or acquisitions would not be the gauge of success for The New World's inhabitants. Rather, with limited space, each citizen subsisted on the bare minimum of possessions. It would be a much different way of life. On Earth, you could reap the rewards of your labor—and that was the point of existence. But A-Dub and Uncle Ray had never lived to have things. They lived happily because of their relationships and by creating a sense of community among their friends. Their decision to live on The New World would change his strategies for their current investments, but that would have to wait for another day. Today's focus was on another matter: the new money.

He turned his attention to research, knowing he may not have liberty with the entire amount. That fact caused him to concentrate on A-Dub and Uncle Ray's share, which he calculated at around $103 million. He considered additional mutual funds, a conservative way to go. He determined this group of lottery winners would more likely agree that their money be used for socially responsible investments. He knew they weren't as interested in how much their money made them as they were in promoting good with their money. He remembered reading a prospectus from The Bank of The World. He typed in their web address.

The organization had been around since the Second World War, established to help rebuild a large portion of Europe after the devastation during that war. After it had fulfilled that function, The Bank of The World changed its mission. In the late 20th century, it provided leveraged loans for developing countries when societies demanded a higher quality of life for all people. Its primary goal became to eradicate poverty. But its newest goal, and the reason for the prospectus, was to raise capital to loan for the construction of fabricated planets, using The New World technology as a prototype. The New World had everyone thinking in new ways. Since this seemed to fit nicely into A-Dub and Uncle Ray's plans, he decided to recommend that a large portion of their winnings be invested with The Bank of the World.

After this decision, he was ready to move onto the next challenge. He liked the stock market and the thrill of the chase for money, so he would suggest investing 90% conservatively, but reserving 10% for something more risky. He argued with himself that 10% would be a "responsible" amount, even though it was over $10 million. The hottest investment opportunity in the stock market was rare earth minerals. Years earlier, when John first developed an interest in investment opportunities, oil dominated. As he began to invest heavily in the early 21st century, water was the hot opportunity. Now, the century was flying by, and minerals were the opportune commodity. All the current technologies depended upon them. The U.S. had fought a war over Afghanistan after the world's largest supplies of rare earth mineral deposits were discovered there. That conflict had paved the way for the capitalization of that country, and global enterprises swooped in to construct mining operations.

He looked into a few of them to assess their strengths and weaknesses, and found a company that mined not only in Afghanistan but in Montana as well. The Peabody Mineral Corporation and Subsidiaries looked like a solid investment. Peabody was mining and selling rare earth minerals to international companies who used them for everything from hybrid cars to military weapons. Their operation was mid-sized, so John's investment with them would be substantial. He looked into the class of stock that had ownership rules attached. Maybe his investment would be enough to give him a major vote in their business affairs. He would eventually need something else to do, anyway. Playing on an international level with these kinds of goods promised a lot of power.

The day had slipped away. John had not taken a break for lunch or dinner. He barely looked up when his assistant announced she was leaving for the day. He was completely absorbed in his research. At 11:00 p.m., his phone rang. It was Treeny. He glanced at the clock as he answered.

"Hey, babe. Didn't realize it was so late."

"Hi, Johnnie. I just called to say goodnight. I can't wait up any longer. I got carry-out from Puccini's if you want something to eat when you get home."

"Oh, thanks, I haven't eaten all day. I guess I am a little hungry."

"Well, goodnight."

"Sorry . . . again. I couldn't find a stopping place today, but I guess this is it." He yawned loudly and pushed his chair away from his desk, "I'm on my way home."

"I'll see you in the morning . . . and thanks for the flowers."

"I love you."

"I know."

Click.

CHAPTER 10

The Chinle hospital in Arizona was a two story concrete structure with barred windows. The reception room, meagerly furnished, was dimly lit by flickering florescent bulbs. The aging art graphics painted on the mint green walls echoed the ancient history of the Navajo people. The tan vinyl floors camouflaged the sand that continually blew in from the desert. It was especially hot this Tuesday evening in June. Ray and Wilma had checked in at the sparsely staffed nurses' station to locate Jake's room. Now they stood in his doorway, looking at the many machines wired to Jake.

"Oh, Ray, this brings back some bad memories."

"I know, Wilma. But he came through then and he'll come through again."

A familiar deep voice with a southern drawl came from behind them, "Looks bad, don't it?"

Ray and Wilma turned at the same time. Jake had appropriately described Jimmy as "mountain man meets basketball player." He was over 6'6", with short-cropped curly red hair and a long red beard. He was dressed in athletic shorts, flip-flops, and a tee shirt from Navajo Nation College.

"You must be Jimmy," said Ray, extending his hand. "You're just like Jake described you."

As Jimmy reached out to shake Ray's hand, he said, "Wish I could make it all better, but he's got God on his side. He's alive and he shouldn't be."

"Yeah. This is not the first time," said Wilma. "He's lived through a lot of bad things. I guess this is just one more." She dropped her head, slowly shaking it from side to side as she whispered, "What's it gonna take?"

"Yep," said Ray, "this brings back memories of the football days. All those contraptions wired to him, making his heart pump and everything . . ."

"How 'bout a cup of coffee for you two?" asked Jimmy. "There's a coffee shop right here in the hospital."

It was 6:00 p.m. and it had been a long travel day for Wilma and Ray. The two-hour time difference from Chicago to Albuquerque made extra demands on their stamina, but their concern for Jake had kept them going. The early Tuesday flight from Midway Airport took them directly to Albuquerque, where they rented a car and drove four and a half hours across the hot Arizona desert to Chinle. This was the first time either had been on the Navajo Indian reservation. They had only seen Jake twice in the last five years: once when he came to Cedar Lake around the time he decided to find his roots and return to the land of his ancestors, and again three years ago when he came home for Christmas. He called frequently, but the conversations were brief and didn't include much news about his life. Wilma and Ray knew very little, but they perceived a lot.

"I sure could use some coffee. How 'bout you, Wilma?" said Ray.

"You two go ahead. I'm going to stay with Jake. I just need to look at him for a while." Wilma entered the room and stood by Jake's side while Ray and Jimmy left for the coffee shop.

Wilma carefully inspected all of the tubes, wires, and machines attached to Jake. In spite of the apparatuses she could tell he had maintained his striking physique. He looked Navajo with his shoulder length black hair graying at the temples. His lifestyle hadn't yet taken a toll on his smooth dark reddish skin. She cringed as she looked at the left side of his face, concealed by gauze. It was the same side hit during his football injury. As she stood gazing, one of the machines began beeping, at first very slowly, then gaining speed, reaching an urgent pace. Wilma ran out into the hall to call for a nurse, but saw one already approaching the room.

"Please, ma'am, stand out of the way," she urged Wilma.

"What's going on?" questioned Wilma as she followed the nurse back into Jake's room.

"It's the brain activity monitor," said the nurse. "This could be good news. That means thoughts are beginning again. It could be something like dreaming. It may mean the swelling is going down." She reached over to the machine and turned on a printer that began to spew a narrow strip of paper with a graph printed on it. "This will show us his brain activity and the doctor will analyze it." The nurse checked Jake's heart rate and temperature, and noted them on a chart. "Excuse me, ma'am, but are you a relative?"

"Yes, I'm Jake's mom. His father and I just arrived from Indiana."

"Then it's okay to be in here but please stay clear of all the equipment. If they beep again, we'll hear them at the nurse's station and come to see what's happening. Go ahead and make yourself as comfortable as you can in that chair in the corner," the nurse offered before exiting the room.

"God, I hope you're doing a miracle," said Wilma aloud as she settled into the chair by the window and continued to watch, not knowing exactly what was happening. Jake's fingers began to move . . . then his hands started twitching.

*   *   *

A doctor dressed in a white lab coat entered the room. "Jake, I'm Dr. Shammah. I want to let you know you're going to be alright."

Jake tried to open his eyes, but the bandages restricted them from opening. He managed to form thoughts despite his condition. *Doesn't sound Navajo. Wonder where he's from. Probably Middle East.*

"You're right, Jake," said the doctor. "It's an ancient name, Hebrew, and it means 'I Am There.'"

Disoriented, Jake questioned himself: *Did I speak out loud? Am I just imagining this? Am I dead?*

"Jake, we are communicating in another realm. It transcends the ability you currently possess in your conscious mind. However, your subconscious is able to communicate this way. When you first learned to pray, you understood this."

"Pray?" questioned Jake. "I haven't prayed since I was about eighteen. Nobody was listening so I stopped. It was pointless."

"No one's prayers go unheard, Jake."

"What's the point of praying?" asked Jake.

Ignoring Jake's question, Dr. Shammah said, "I have something I would like you to watch. Do you mind?"

"Uh, yeah, but in case you didn't notice, I can't see."

"You'll be able to see this," reassured the doctor.

"Okay, if you say so. What's it about?"

"It's your life." Dr. Shammah pulled a flash drive out of his lab coat pocket. Another doctor entered the room with a digital player on a rolling cart. "This is Dr. Yeshua. He's my right hand. He has something else for you to watch."

Might be Navajo, might be another Middle Easterner, I suppose, thought Jake.

"Yes, I too have an ancient Hebrew name. Are you ready to watch your life, Jake?" asked Dr. Yeshua.

"Looks like I don't have a choice."

"You always have a choice. That's how you were made, with choices and decisions to make, but you also have the ability to choose well over choosing badly. In this case, choosing to watch this would be choosing well."

His soothing voice convinced Jake that yielding would be a benefit.

"I'm ready."

"Please put on this enhancement headphone, Jake. It will allow you to experience emotions as the visuals guide you in remembering things from your past." Jake put the headphones on and the visual images began to roll.

Jake, eight years old, sitting on his bed in a dimly lit room, is looking out the window at a bright distant star. "God, help my mommy. I don't want her to die. She helps me every day to do things I can't do. My daddy loves her, too. Me and Johnnie need a mommy. Please, God, help her."

The scene fades out and new images begin.

Jake and Johnnie are in their messy kitchen. It's night and Jake is at the stove, boiling water. On the counter is a boxed macaroni and cheese dinner. Johnnie is doing his homework at the kitchen table. Jake, waiting for the water to boil, picks up a wooden yardstick, wielding it like a sword. Their father stumbles in the back door.

"Hey, boys," he slurs as he tussles their heads. "Sorry, I'm late. I stopped at Sonnies' and lost track of time." Jake looks at the clock above the kitchen sink: 10:00 p.m. Juan goes into the living room where he kicks off his shoes and lays down on the sofa. Jake and Johnnie look at each other and shrug as they continue what they were doing. After eating the macaroni and cheese dinner, they leave their dishes on the table and the pan on the stove, and start to bed. Their father is sleeping on the sofa. Jake goes over to him and tries to wake him to go to bed but his father shoos him away and rolls over. Jake goes to his room, but before he crawls into bed, he looks out his bedroom window at the same bright star and says, "God, take care of my daddy. I need my daddy now more than ever. Without my mommy, it's been hard. Me and Johnnie gotta do the things she used to do and it's kind of lonely when daddy stays out so late."

The scene fades out and new images begin.

It is a crisp Sunday in late November. Jake is sitting at Aunt Wilma's kitchen table. The satisfying aroma of delicious pancakes with maple syrup fills the air. He is talking to Uncle Ray about what makes the best fishing lures. Johnnie is playing a handheld video game. Aunt Wilma is whistling a song Jake recognizes from church as she cleans up the pancake griddle. "You boys better finish up. Church starts in about thirty minutes."

"Okay," says Jake, finishing his pancakes. He runs up the stairs to his room to dress. He quickly throws on jeans, a T-shirt, and tennis shoes then runs out the back door to his father's house next door. Coming in the back door, he calls out, "Hey, dad, you want to come to church with us today?"

He finds his dad asleep on the living room sofa. Jake wiggles in beside him. His dad tussles Jake's head and yawns. "I think I'm going to St. Sonnies' today, son. My god lives in a bottle these days, not within the walls of the church building. Besides, it's Sunday and I'm looking forward to spending the whole day with him. Why don't you do the same? Go ahead and go to church where A-Dub and Ray's God lives, you know, outta respect for them, then go fishing or hunting or something where your god lives." Jake hears Uncle Ray calling his name, so he quickly tussles his dad's head and runs out the back door.

The scene fades out and new images begin.

Jake opens the door to Sonnies' and boldly enters. He is a junior in high school. It's game day and he's slated to start as a running back for the football team that evening. In the faintly lit room, he sees his father sitting at the bar with a half empty bottle of something gold colored and a small glass in front of him. The bar tender growls "It's you again. You know you can't be in here. You ain't of age."

Jake growls back, "I'm only going to be a minute."

"Don't you take my paying customer out of here again. I gotta make a living like everybody else," roars the bartender.

Jake's dad looks toward the commotion, "Hey, come here, Jake, have a seat. Whatcha need son?"

Jake eyes the bartender as he takes a seat next to his dad. "Dad, it's Homecoming tonight and they say there's going to be some college scouts at the game. I was wondering if you would come to the game. It's gonna be a good one."

"Uh . . . I guess I could come. What time does it start?" slurs his dad.

"In about an hour," said Jake. "Thanks, Dad. It means a lot to me. I better get going. The coach wants us to be there a little early. Some game strategy stuff, you know." He tussles his dad's head.

Before leaving Sonnies' Jake turns to the bartender, "You wanna make a sale? Then bring the man some coffee."

The scene fades out and new images begin.

Jake is on the sideline, turning to scan the crowd. As the game begins, Jake is determined to do his best for his audience of one, his dad. This would be the first game his dad ever attended. Halftime comes and in spite of continually glancing at the crowd, Jake doesn't see his dad. In the locker room, Jake's coach gives the pep talk that Jake's heard a dozen times before so his mind wanders, still hoping his dad is in the crowd. As the second half begins, Jake spots Johnnie at the fence behind the players and breaks the rules by talking to him. "Did you see Dad?"

"Dad? Are you kidding me?"

"No, I saw him this afternoon and he said he would come. Could you look around and see if he's here?" asked Jake.

"Uh, sure, Jake. It would be a big surprise to me, but I'll check around. I'll let you know later." Johnnie heads to the concession stand to ask if anyone has seen his dad.

After the game, Johnnie waits for Jake by the locker room doors. "Jake," he said shaking his head, "he didn't come. I looked everywhere and asked everyone, but no one saw him. I went to Sonnies' to see if he was there. The bartender said he fell off his stool, so he put him in a cab to take him home about thirty minutes ago. Sorry, man."

Jake doesn't say a word. He just turns and walks away.

Again the scene fades out and new images begin.

Jake is sitting at the top of the water tower on the edge of town, bottle of vodka in hand, looking up at a bright star. "God, I'm trading you in. You never hear me. My mom's gone and now my dad. I needed them," he cried. "I needed a mom and a dad." He takes a big gulp from the bottle and coughs. "Dad, since you won't join me, I'll join you."

The scene fades out and new images begin.

Jake is in the NFL playoffs. He feels mean tonight. He is concentrating all of his anger on winning this game. His team is in possession of the ball. The ball is snapped. The quarterback fades back and looks for an open receiver. Jake runs long, close to the sideline, and is wide open to receive the ball. He sees a blurry ball as it hurls through the air. Jake's head struggles to focus, knowing he needs a clean catch so he can run the ball into the end zone. *I thought those pain meds would wear off by now.* Hands in the air, he jumps high and the ball grazes his fingertips. Whap! A defensive back comes behind him out of nowhere—and the force stops him like a stone wall. Jake's helmet flies off . . . just before he hits the ground, head first.

The scene fades out and new images begin.

Jake is in the waiting room of an Imaging Center. He looks at the clock, it's 3:30. He approaches the reception counter to speak to the person in charge. "I had a 3:00 appointment," he says in a loud angry voice. "I don't like to wait. When I make an appointment, I do not expect to wait."

"I'm sorry, Mr. Minda. The patient before you needed additional scans and it is taking a little longer," explained the young lady behind the counter. "If you will wait here, I'll find out how much longer it will be."

"I'm not waiting," he hollers. He swipes his arm across the counter, knocking informational brochures and the check-in list to the floor. "I'm tired of waiting. Waiting for bad news again." He turns to leave, but before he exits, he takes a chair and throws it across the room, just missing the nurse coming to escort him for his scan. The nurse speaks, "Mr. Minda, the doctor is very hopeful this time." Jake blows through the door and out into the parking lot.

The key fob opens his Hummer 2 Sport Utility Truck. He peels rubber as he leaves the parking lot, heading to his home away from home. Pulling into the Westin in downtown Dallas, he throws his keys at the valet. "Take care of it, will ya?"

He goes into the lounge. "Give me a triple today, Gravél," he commands the bartender. "Might as well get a head start." He chugs the whiskey like water. He commanded, "Gimme another," breathing a little easier. "Give me peace, god," he says, gripping his next drink. "Now I know why you made this your god, dad. Everything goes a little easier when you're in charge." He chugs his next drink and settles into a barstool. "Hell, Gravél, it would have been the same bad news anyway. Why keep wasting my time?"

"Yeah, you're probably right," Louis Gravél says, picking up on the conversation Jake had started. "The idiots! Who needs 'em?"

"Not me, that's for sure. They can take a flying leap. I'm tired of living with these restrictions. I'm climbing outta my skin waiting for something to happen. I'm gonna start making things happen for myself. I been thinking, Louie. How would you like to be partners?"

The scene fades out and the screen goes black.

Dr. Shammah speaks. "Jake, as you can see, your life has been recorded. I have witnessed every action and every thought. These are just excerpts. However, there are things that you have been unaware of that have influenced your life. Your disappointments have led you to be an angry man and you have projected your anger onto every relationship you have. I am so sorry for your disappointments, Jake. I tried to help you understand things better, but you shut me out. You have chosen to live for the gods who suck the life out of you and give you nothing in return But you have also realized the futility in choosing a god who doesn't love you back, and I believe you are ready to listen now. Watch as Dr. Yeshua plays something from a different point of view."

CHAPTER 11

Ray and Jimmy returned from the coffee shop, moseying down the dim corridor. As they approached Jake's room, they could hear excited voices and activity. They picked up their pace and hurried to his room. The monitors attached to Jake beeped wildly as two nurses and a doctor hovered over his bed. One nurse wrote furiously on her chart as the other two tensely called out numbers. The medical team, focused on Jake, didn't notice Ray and Jimmy. Wilma, planted in the corner chair with her feet curled up under her, appeared strangely calm, given the circumstances. She held up her hand, motioning Ray and Jimmy to stop at the door, then shushed them by holding her finger to her lips. Folding her hands together and bowing her head, she indicated they needed to pray.

*   *   *

Dr. Yeshua, standing at the foot of Jake's hospital bed, began speaking. "Jake, you have just watched your life from *your* point of view. Now we want you to watch your life from our point of view." He turned and walked to the rolling cart. "You won't need the headphones for this. Since you have not experienced these events, none of your past emotions are attached to the viewing." Jake's emotions had been shaken by the enhancement headphone experience and he showed relief to not wear them again. The doctor patiently waited as Jake slowly removed the headphones. He gently took the headphones from Jake and returned them to the rolling cart. He pushed the play button and the screen brightened as he added, "You will, however, experience first-time emotions over what you view."

The first image comes into view. Wilma and Ray are leaving a hospital. Wilma is crying and Ray has his arm around her shoulders. "I don't think she's going to make it, Ray. I begged her so many times to quit smoking. She would just tell me she liked it too much to quit." Wilma's sobs increase as she chokes out her words. "She knew where it would lead . . . I am angry that she chose smoking over the love of her boys . . . What a selfish habit! Mostly, I'm sad for those boys. What are they going to do without a mom?"

Ray consoles her as he removes his hand from her shoulder and holds tightly to her hand. "We'll do whatever we have to do, Wilma."

The scene fades out and new images begin.

Wilma and Ray are standing under a tall tree in a cemetery on a drizzly day in early spring. As the last car pulls away, they walk to an open grave and Wilma tosses a rose onto the casket. "Goodbye, Sis. I'll miss you." They turn and walk hand in hand to their car. "I am so sad, Ray. My heart breaks for those boys. Did you see their little faces today? What can we do to help them?" Wilma asks through her tears.

"We'll do whatever we need to do, Wilma," says Ray as he opens the car door for her. The drive to her sister's and brother-in-law's house is quiet. As they pull into the drive, Wilma turns to Ray.

"Ray, what do you think about moving here to Cedar Lake?"

Ray doesn't hesitate. "I've been thinking that myself. It's only a forty-five minute drive to work. I could do that until I find a job here. Those boys are going to need you." He adds, "I've always liked that house next door. Maybe the owners would sell it to us."

"Oh, Ray. That's why I love you so much. You always know the right thing to say and do. I know you love those boys as much as I do and they're going to need you as much as they're going to need me."

"Wilma, you go on into the house. I'm going next door to talk to those folks about buying their house."

The scene fades out and new images begin.

The sun is bright as Ray is seen in his "tinker shed" behind the house. Jake, bursting through the door, interrupts his whistling. "Hey, Uncle Ray. I got an idea for a new fishing lure. Can you help me make it?"

"What, right now?" chuckles Uncle Ray. He puts down his hammer and gladly allows the interruption of a ten-year-old boy's joyous spontaneity. They work for an hour before they test the lure at the lake. An afternoon of fishing yields enough fish for supper.

Jake opens the kitchen door and hollers, "Hey, Aunt Willy. Me and Uncle Ray caught some fish for supper. We're gonna clean 'em, and you said if we cleaned 'em, you'd cook 'em."

Wilma comes to the back door smiling. "Sure, we can. Want some hush puppies, too?" she asks Jake. "I know how much you like them, better than the fish I imagine, and by the way . . . that's Uncle Ray and I. Always use proper English."

"I know," says Jake. "I just like to say it the other way." He hesitates a minute, then asks, "Can I ask Dad to come?"

"Sure, Jake, but I haven't seen his car since about noon. He's probably in town."

Jake drops his head and says quietly to himself, "You mean at Sonnies'."

The scene fades out and new images begin.

The phone is ringing and Uncle Ray answers formally, not recognizing the number on the caller ID. "Smith residence."

"Oh, hi, Coach," Ray responds. "What?! Scouts from Purdue? Does Jake know?" He hangs up the phone and goes to the front yard where Wilma is planting mums for the fall season. "Hey, good news! Jake's coach just called. He wanted us to know there will be scouts from Purdue at the game tonight to watch Jake. Apparently he is getting noticed by a Big Ten school."

"Yeehaw!" Wilma exclaims as she jumps up. She grabs Ray and they start dancing around. After they settle down, she whispers in Ray's ear, "Maybe this will make him happy."

"I only hope," says Ray. "He's been pretty down."

Again the scene fades and new images begin.

Wilma and Ray are standing in the doorway of Jake's hospital room. "Ray, what are we going to do to help him?" asks Wilma.

"We'll do whatever it takes, Wilma. He needs us as much now as he ever has," says Ray.

"I can't leave him here like this. There's no one to love him through this. I have to stay here. I hope Mr. Bledshaw understands. If I have to quit my job, then we'll have to trust God with our needs."

"Let's not get too hasty. I don't think Mr. Bledshaw will accept your resignation. Maybe you should ask for a leave of absence and he can get someone to fill in for you until all this settles down."

"You're right Ray. I always get a little ahead of myself," Wilma sighs.

"Now let's get you checked into the hotel next door."

The scene fades out and new images begin.

Wilma and Ray are in the kitchen, taking pies out of the oven. Wilma appears a little down. Ray asks, "Do you want me to call him so you can wish him a Happy Thanksgiving?" Wilma's face brightens as Ray dials the phone and hands it to Wilma.

It's 9:00 a.m. and the phone rings in Jake's plush high rise in downtown Dallas. "Who the ?@#! is that?" Jake swears aloud and struggles to find the phone on his nightstand. "What!" he demands as he answers the phone.

"Happy Thanksgiving, Jake," comes Wilma's sweet voice over the phone.

"Oh, sorry A-Dub," says Jake, embarrassed by his curtness. He clears his throat. "Happy Thanksgiving to you, too. You having a big dinner today?"

"We're going down to the church for a noon meal. The girls and I made all the pies and we're going to help serve. Everybody in town is invited. It's our fifth year for this event and we're expecting around 300 people."

"Sounds nice," yawns Jake as he rolls over onto someone lying next to him. "What's Uncle Ray up to?"

"He and some of the men have been roasting turkeys on spits over open fires all night. Something new they cooked up," chuckles Wilma, as if amused by her own pun. "Well, I just wanted you to know we always think of you and miss you during the holidays."

"Yeah, I miss you guys, too," Jake lies as he takes a gulp of liquor from the bottle on his nightstand.

"Do you think you will be able to come for Christmas this year?" asks Wilma.

"I'm sure going to try. I've got a big deal in the works, though. A big investment opportunity. I've been talking to Johnnie about it. And, get this. I'm moving to Arizona. I'm tired of waiting around for football to be my life again. I've got to move on. I'll talk to you about this later, though. I gotta get going." He quickly ends his conversation because his bed guest is awake and ready to get the day started.

Wilma stands quietly for a moment, still holding the phone. "God, I know You have a plan for him and as long as You're not giving up on him, then I won't either."

The scene fades out and the screen goes black.

Dr. Yeshua is speaking. "As you can see, Jake, your prayers as a boy *were* answered. We made sure you had a mom and a dad. Wilma and Ray loved you more than either of your biological parents did. Your biological parents chose selfish behavior over selfless love for you and your brother. They didn't truly understand love. True love sacrifices selfish desires for the best interest of others. Wilma and Ray sacrificed the life they might have had for the love of you and your brother. They showed love with their life choices. They have always been there to support and encourage you throughout your life."

Tears welled up in Jake's bandaged eyes. He had held back his emotions until he could no longer control them. "I have been so wrong all my life! God, You had me surrounded with love and I was too blind to see what I had. I wanted it the way *I* wanted it. I didn't see what You had for me. I have been an angry man because of it and my anger has affected everyone, even strangers. I was too selfish to see what was really happening."

Dr. Shammah and Dr. Yeshua came to his bed, one on either side. Dr. Shammah laid his hands on Jake's heart and Dr. Yeshua put his hands on Jake's head. Jake immediately felt a warm sensation swell from the inside of his body. Images came to his mind of a beautiful, peaceful garden that welcomed him with a familiar floral smell. Jake was struggling to let go and give into the vision. A man dressed in a white lab coat came walking up a path. "I am Dr. Ruach—yes, also a Hebrew name. I am here to explain a concept to you. You, as well as all other humans, have been created with a capacity for three dimensions. They are spirit, body, and soul.

"You've met Dr. Shammah. He is the doctor in charge of your spirit. It is the essence of who you are. Your spirit has been created in the likeness of God. This part of you desires to identify with God and His ways. Dr. Yeshua is the doctor in charge of your body, the vehicle your spirit uses to move about the earth. He was the first flesh-born spirit son of God; he was given a body to walk the earth, which makes him an expert of the body. His objective is to teach you that your bodies are to be used for doing God's purpose on the earth. However, there is a battle for the use of the body. The body has strong needs and can also be used for fulfilling selfish purposes.

"So again, I am Dr. Ruach—the doctor in charge of your soul. The soul is the place where you make decisions that will satisfy the spirit part of you as well as the urges of your body. It is the part of you where desires and creativity dwell—your passions, if you will. Your personality and expression of life are defined by the choices you make with your soul.

"In the order of God's world, it takes two in agreement with each other so that a thing can be accomplished. So . . . when your soul agrees with your spirit, it controls what you do with your body. But, if the soul agrees with the selfish urges of the body, then the spirit part of you will be squelched. However, guilt is the built-in barometer of the spirit to alert you that a change needs to occur. The decision to follow your spirit—or the decision to follow the selfish nature of your body—is made by your soul. Since I am the doctor responsible for that part of you, I have some instruction for you. When you find yourself being selfish, self-centered, or self-seeking in your desires, it's a sign for you to find out what the spirit part of you desires. The spirit man, or the God part, wants you to identify with His ways. Those are the ways of love. Love is not self-seeking. It seeks to encourage and uplift others. Do you understand, Jake?"

Jake, not needing to communicate with words, formed his thought which was transferred to Dr. Ruach at the speed of light. "Are you saying the soul is the bad boy part of me?"

"No, Jake. Quite the contrary. It's the most amazing part of you. It's the part of you that *is* you: creative, imaginative, original, innovative. That's where Dr. Shammah's work is showcased. What I am saying is the soul is where you decide how you will live your life. Will you help God with His plan on the earth or will you use all that He has given you to help only yourself? If you decide to use what God has given you for His purposes, you can be a part of something truly amazing, and you will be completely satisfied with eternal life. If you use what He's given you to fulfill your own desires, then that's what you get—and that's all you get—and life is over. It's your choice, Jake. After today, you won't have the excuse of ignorance. These recorded events and your experience with me have given you insight into the world you have chosen to ignore. Remember to pray. It's your way to communicate with God to find out what the game plan is." Dr. Ruach winked . . . and then he was gone.

*   *   *

"CODE BLUE, CODE BLUE! Our patient is in cardiac arrest!" one of the nurses called out loudly as she ran into the hall.

"Bring the cart!" Immediately, they jerked Jake's hospital gown away and held the shock paddles to his chest. "Clear?" asked the doctor in a calm voice. "Clear," was the reply. BAM! The volts ran through him. "Again," ordered the doctor after a short wait. BAM!

Wilma continued to sit quietly in the corner chair as Ray and Jimmy stood in the doorway. All were praying.

*　*　*

"Good work, Dr. Yeshua," said Dr. Shammah.

"That gets to me every time I replace a heart of stone with a heart of flesh," said Dr. Yeshua. "But it's always worth it when the old nature dies and a new nature begins. I guess the rest is up to you, Dr. Ruach."

Dr. Ruach smiled and said, "I think everything is going to be alright now."

CHAPTER 12

Mentally exhausted, John chose to have his car valet parked, a homeowner's benefit, minus the tip, of their 15th floor high rise overlooking Lake Michigan. Every time he stepped off the elevator onto their floor, he swelled with pride at being able to afford this kind of luxury. Six thousand square feet at this address translated to six million bucks. Treeny contributed too, quite a bit, but this kind of extravagance was not important to her. John needed an impressive address. As much as he tried to act humble, most of his acquisitions were for image building. He needed them for the approval and admiration of others. Treeny, on the other hand, didn't need approval from others, but she attracted it by her genuine nature. John had battled constantly living in someone else's shadow. First, it was Jake while they were growing up, now it was Treeny. No matter what he achieved, or how much he acquired, he was overshadowed.

As he rode up the elevator, he imagined the status this money would bring. *They will notice me now. I am going to be a multi-millionaire. I can give to charities and get my picture in the paper. The church will get a large donation . . . maybe they'll even build a new wing and name it after me . . .*

It was 11:30 when he arrived home. The large living room was lit with a soft glow from the city lights through the expanse of windows.

"Puccini's," he said as he went into the kitchen. Upon opening the refrigerator door, he was greeted with the robust scent of garlic. He grabbed the distinctive red and white checkered cardboard container from his favorite Italian restaurant and retrieved a fork from the silverware drawer. He jabbed the utensil into the center of the pasta and wound it around until he had more than a mouthful. Mmmm . . . Spaghetti Bolognese: one of Treeny's favorites. He finished her cold leftovers, went to the living room, and let his body free fall onto the feather cushioned leather sofa. He was about to voice activate the TV, when he noticed an open book on the coffee table. It was the only thing out of its place.

He flipped on the table lamp and discovered it was the Bible. A yellow highlighted passage drew his attention. "*__For the word of God is living and active. Sharper than any double edged sword, it penetrates even to dividing soul and spirit, joints and marrow; it judges the thoughts and attitudes of the heart.__*" It could have been his imagination—or his stomach responding to the garlic—but when he read the words, a sharp pain actually did pierce him in the heart. He rubbed his chest with his hand. He learned toward the coffee table to get a closer look at the words. He read them again, slowly. He felt his temperature rise as his thoughts raced. Reading the verse was like facing a judge, convicting him of the façade he had built. He was guilty of managing a public image of a nice guy, but he knew he made every decision based on his own best interest. A battle ensued within as he began to defend himself. *I am a good person. I spend a lot of my time at church and give a lot of money, too. I take care of Treeny. I keep in touch with Uncle Ray and A-Dub. I do everything right.*

"But do you love Me more than these things?" came a soft voice from somewhere.

John jumped up and looked around, expecting to see Treeny. But there was no Treeny. The voice was so soft, he figured he must have imagined it. When it was clear he was alone, he walked into the guest bathroom and threw cold water on his face. He looked in on Treeny before going back to the living room to turn on the television. He took off his shoes, hung his clothes over the back of a chair, lay down on the sofa, and pulled a throw over himself.

Sleep introduced itself, and with little resistance, quickly took over.

*   *   *

Johnnie was in his upstairs bedroom at Uncle Ray and A-Dub's in Cedar Lake. *Jake might be able to play football, but I get better grades. I'll probably get an academic scholarship and Jake will stay around here his whole life—fishing.* He was looking in the mirror, combing his hair. *I'm better looking, too. Might even try to steal your girlfriend tonight. Just to show you I can. Wouldn't that tick you off? Ha!*

A man dressed in faded jeans and a white polo shirt appeared in the open doorway to Johnnie's bedroom. "Mind if I come in?" he asked.

"Where did *you* come from?" asked John.

"From everywhere." He walked into the room and sat on the bed. "I've just been listening to your secret life."

"What secret life?"

"The secret life of your mind," the man replied. "It's not as nice as you appear to be. You have a lot of people fooled, but if they could see you the way I see you, they would say you have a real problem with your brother."

John was offended by the remark and didn't know if he should respond.

"Jealous?" the man said.

"No! He's a loser. A pompous loser! He's got hate written all over him. And real anger issues," said John.

"Need a mirror, my friend?"

"Who are you, anyway?"

"I'm your conscience. You know, the thing that keeps you doing the right thing. You're going to have to watch yourself. Jealousy caused the first murder, you know. Remember Cain and Abel? Just a warning."

John woke with a start, struggling for clarity. The dream was a jumbled memory of his night with Selena Owens and a stranger who hadn't existed in real life. He rose from the sofa and stumbled into the kitchen for a drink of water. He rubbed his head with both hands as if it would wipe away the memory of the dream. Returning to the sofa, he stared at the television, continuing to play 24-hour weather, until the weariness took over again.

*   *   *

John was in the Episcopal Church in the heart of downtown Chicago, preparing for a special session of the board to increase the size of the historic landmark building. His reason for being involved with this project was to get himself plenty of exposure in the press. His was sure his financial influence with the people at this meeting would get him the vote he wanted. *Got the girl, got the job, got the car, and got the right address. Now I'm going to get the vote. Money always gets its way.*

The man in the jeans and white polo shirt appeared in the doorway. "Hey, friend, I see it's getting the best of you."

"You again? What are you doing here? I'll be moderating a meeting in a few minutes. Don't have time for you," shooing the man with one hand as he gathered some papers with the other. He strutted into the conference room, where twelve men were seated at a large table, and began to preside over the order of business.

When the meeting ended, John was superficially apologizing to a humble man of small stature whose disagreement with John stemmed from having the people's best interests at heart, not simply the architecture of the building.

"I'm sorry things didn't go your way, Mr. Sweeny," John offered insincerely, "but we're well into a new century now and we have to look at things differently."

"Maybe you're right, John. I have to move aside and let you young ones take the lead. Just don't forget why we're a church. It's not about buildings or programs, or how we look or sound, but it's about caring for people and being God's hand in the earth. I

just hope we don't forget to spend our money on the *right* things."
He tipped his hat to John as he left.

Yeah, time to move over, old man. Our building is an important architectural icon for this city. Our government will take care of the people.

The mysterious man appeared in the doorway again. "Would it have done any harm to respectfully consider his thoughts instead of defending your personal agenda?" Before he turned to leave, he smiled and said, "What does it profit a man if he gains the whole world and loses his soul in the process?"

John woke abruptly as he rolled off the sofa and hit the floor with a thud. *What a night!* He struggled to get to his feet and went into the bathroom. After completing his business, he was back on the sofa and quickly asleep again.

*   *   *

John was having dinner with Uncle Ray and Aunt Wilma, struggling with the small talk. His thoughts dominated his attention. *I am a good person and I will do good things with this money.* He was trying to convince himself that he had noble motives about the lottery money, soon to be in his charge. *Yes, I will give a portion to the church, but I don't know about the required 10%. That's a lot. Anyway, with The New World, I don't know how many congregations will still be meeting. The church buildings will probably turn into museums or community-use facilities and the Christians who stay will probably meet in houses. Churches won't need to raise money anymore.*

As Aunt Wilma was signing the document making John trustee of the winning ticket, he saw the man with the jeans and white polo shirt come in through the back door. The man propped himself against the wall and folded his arms over his chest.

"What about you, John? Are you interested in going to The New World?"

"Me? Uh, probably not. Somebody has to act responsibly with this money. I mean, you know, do the right thing with it."

"And that somebody is you?"

"I sure don't know who else it would be," John snapped.

He was beginning to be a little uncomfortable with this man's demeanor. *No one has ever questioned me like this before. Who does he think he is anyway?*

"You don't know who I am?"

"Can you read my mind?"

"I can discern you thoughts. It's my job to help you see things more clearly. Help you understand yourself better. You see, John, there is a big difference between good and God."

"I always thought good and God were the same."

"Yet good can be acted out for selfish purposes. In other words, a person can perform good deeds, but his motivation is not for others, it is for himself. The act may draw attention and feed his pride, thereby nullifying the good deed in God's eyes. Selfish behavior is counter to Godly-motivated behavior. God promises to look out for your needs when you look out for the needs of others. Now in your case, the jealousy you have had toward your brother all these years has fueled your good deeds. Your showy lifestyle is to gain the attention you felt you never had while growing up. You have always believed you were in Jake's shadow. All of your good deeds have been for selfish reasons. This has become a way of life for you. You've used good deeds to manipulate your way into situations. God looks at the heart of a person, not only his deeds. He knows you in your deepest places and He is most concerned with your motives. He wants your heart, not your behavior. Men are concerned with behavior. That's all they see. But God sees your heart."

"You mean all these years of serving in the church, doing the right thing, giving money to good causes . . . that doesn't mean anything to God?"

"Those acts have helped a lot of people—even you, because you chose a good path. But God wants the rest of you. He wants your motivation to be the love of others, not the love of yourself.

He wants your good deeds to be His hand on the earth. When you accomplish only the things you desire, you limit what God can do. His ways and thoughts are much higher than yours are and you cannot accomplish His purpose unless your motivation becomes His motivation. That motivation must come from genuine love and concern for others, because no one can be good on his own. Otherwise, we will worship and adore ourselves for our own good works. That, my friend, is called pride. Besides all that, loving others in this way will heal your hurts. If you try to heal yourself through meeting your own needs by doing good deeds, you will continue to hurt on the inside. When you surrender all of your hurts and ambitions to God, then you can truly love others. It's only when you give your life away that you get a life."

"I don't know what you mean to 'give your life away,'" John wondered.

"Giving your life away simply means you plug into what God is doing in the earth. God has a great plan to redeem the human race from selfishness and that can only happen when we surrender ourselves to live according to his ways. Love is the higher road that transcends selfishness."

"I've never thought about it like that. I thought as long as I did good things, that was what God wanted from me." John paused. "But I'm beginning to see things a little differently. I've been doing good things simply to rescue myself."

"When you do that, you limit what can be done on earth. In a nutshell, John, if everyone would cooperate with God and choose His ways, then His power and influence would be without limits on the earth."

John hung his head. "I'm ashamed. It's like I am looking at myself in the mirror for the first time and see how ugly I am." Looking hopefully at the man, he continued. "I feel like my mind has been expanded to understand a concept that I had never considered. I feel alive for the first time. I've just tossed away a bunch of wrong thinking and allowed it to be replaced with right thinking." With growing conviction, John declared, "I am being changed. Refreshed. Hopeful. Ready to plug into the bigger picture. I know I have a lot to offer and I'm ready to do it God's way, not my way. I have fought selfishness but I thought my good deeds were enough to make things right. I've concentrated so much on making myself do the right things that I haven't been honest with myself to see they've all been motivated by what I could get out of it."

"John, God forgives you. All He needs is your cooperation and I think I'm hearing you say you are giving that to Him now."

"That's right. He has my cooperation. No more selfish ways." John dropped his head and closed his eyes for a moment. When he opened them, the man was gone.

*　　*　　*

John woke with a stream of sunlight beaming in his face. He lay still, contemplating his nocturnal revelations. He allowed them to be real as he went over them in his mind. Shortly, he heard Treeny in the kitchen making coffee, even though she was being quiet as a mouse. He continued to reflect on his dreams, giving into the permanent change in him. He whispered, "God, help me remember last night. Let it never slip away from me."

"Hey, you awake?" Treeny asked sweetly.

"Yeah, I'm awake," he said as he came into the kitchen. "I've had quite an amazing twenty-four hours. I'm not going to be the same guy anymore."

"Oh yeah? Who are you going to be now?" giggled Treeny.

"I'm going to be better, Treeny. I'm going to be motivated by love—not money, power, jealousy, anger, or anything else that would try to be a substitute for love."

Treeny came close to John and snuggled into his chest. "Thank you, God," she whispered as she recalled the Bible passage she had highlighted last night before going to bed.

CHAPTER 13

Ray, Wilma, and Jimmy had slept in the waiting room the night of the dramatic events with Jake. Wilma hadn't wanted to leave the hospital. Early the next morning, as they were waking from a brief rest, a doctor approached them.

"Mr. and Mrs. Smith?"

Wilma stood up as Ray shook the doctor's hand. "That's right. I'm Jake Minda's dad, Ray Smith, and this is his mom, Wilma Smith. How is he this morning?"

"He is conscious. He is out of the coma but still very weak. We would like him to stay another twenty-four to forty-eight hours for observation, just to make sure he's stable."

Wilma melted into Ray's chest. With unspeakable relief, she hugged him tightly. "I knew something was going on, but that cardiac arrest had me concerned." She faced the doctor as she asked, "Is there any heart damage?"

"No, as a matter of fact, his heart is beating as strong as any athlete. I understand he's a professional football player?"

"He was," answered Ray. "He hasn't played professionally in several years. We have been very concerned because he had a head injury that forced him into early retirement. His injury a few nights ago was in the same place where he had the brain bleed that hasn't healed."

The doctor scratched his head. With hesitation, he said, "According to the MRI, there's no sign of a brain bleed. Only contusions and lacerations on his head and shoulder area."

"No sign of a brain bleed?" Wilma was baffled. "How can that be? That's what prevented him from returning to pro football. His doctors in Dallas never released him. He just stopped going for the brain scans. Is it possible that he recovered from this long ago?"

"It's possible," answered the doctor, "but without his records there is no way to know for sure."

Wilma turned to Ray, shaking her head. "Do you think he's been wasting his time for nothing?"

Jimmy politely interrupted, "Excuse me for saying this, ma'am, but it hasn't been a waste of his time. I think he's been finding himself. I know it looks like he's led a pretty crummy life, but I'm a believer that God can use things even when they look bad. I have hoped and prayed that this situation will turn Jake around and that his life will stand for something good. He's been building a reputation with influence that he wouldn't have gotten any other way. I want to show the two of you something. It's on the way to my house, but first we need to go see Jake."

The doctor escorted the three to Jake's room. Immediately Wilma went to his side and stroked his cheek, as if he were a little boy. "Jake, thank God you're alive." Ray came to his other side and took his hand. Jimmy stood at the foot of his bed. "Thank God is right," said Jimmy as he openly continued to give thanks to God.

When Jimmy had said his prayers, Jake smiled and spoke. "I *am* all right. Probably for the first time in my life. Something happened while I was in that coma. I don't know if it was real or if it was a dream, but I know I want to change the way I live my life. I have been living for myself all these years, being angry and dishing out that anger to everyone, even strangers. I don't want to be that guy anymore." He stopped, not because he was out of words, but because his emotions took over.

Sensing his fatigue, Wilma said gently, "We'll come back later, Jake, when you have some strength. You need to rest now."

As they exited the room, the doctor cautioned, "He's under heavy sedation and will probably sleep until late this afternoon or early evening. You should know that it's normal for people to see their lives differently after trauma. But don't worry, he'll probably return to being himself in a few weeks."

Jimmy spoke hastily, "I hope not." He smiled at Wilma and Ray. "Let's go to my house so you can freshen up. I'm anxious for you to meet the little girl, too."

Wilma insisted they call Johnnie before they left the hospital to let him know about Jake.

John's cell phone interrupted his hug with Treeny. The ring tone allowed him to know it was Aunt Wilma. He kissed Treeny on the cheek and said, "I better answer that. A-Dub probably has news of Jake."

"Hello, A-Dub."

"Hi, Johnnie. Good news. Jake is out of the coma and it looks like he's going to be okay."

"How okay? Is there any damage to his head?"

"No, not any. And what's amazing is that there's no sign of his old brain bleed injury either. He only has cuts and bruises from the fight. He even had a heart attack yesterday and there's no sign of damage from that, either."

"A heart attack? What happened?"

Excitedly, Wilma began to explain. "No one knows for sure, but God was definitely there. Shortly after we arrived, the monitors attached to his head began to show signs of brain activity. That was good news, because they were hopeful that he was coming out of his coma. Then the chest monitors started to go crazy. They called in the crash cart and shocked his heart. I was in the room the whole time; Ray was in the coffee shop but got back just in time to pray during the heart attack episode. Jake's friend, Jimmy, was there, too."

"Slow down, A-Dub!"

"I can't help myself, Johnnie. It was a miracle. The room even had a sort of a glow. God was there. I mean, right in the room with us. We all sensed it. And something happened to Jake. I don't know what just yet because he hasn't been able to tell us. But he said he was going to be all right, and he added, all right for the first time in his life. Something good happened. I think this is the change we've all been praying for!"

The phone was silent on John's end.

"Johnnie, did you hear me?"

"Yeah . . . I . . . heard you, A-Dub," he spoke haltingly. "You know what they say about twins, how they experience the same things even though they're separated? Well, I had something happen to me last night and I, too, am going to be all right for the first time in my life."

"What happened, Johnnie?"

"I finally gave up being jealous of Jake and doing good deeds just to be recognized. In a series of dreams, I saw how selfish I've been. I didn't know what was happening at first, but by this morning it was clear. My motivations in life have been all for myself. It's amazing how differently I see things after just one night. I believe God had something to do with it and I know if He did that for me, then He has done that for Jake. Maybe now all of his self-destructive and angry ways will change and the positive influence that we have known he is capable of will emerge."

Tears began to stream down Wilma's face. "Thank-you God for answered prayers," she whispered. "Johnnie, I love you and Jake with all my heart."

"A-Dub, I love you back. I am changing the way I look at things. I don't love you because of what you give to me, I love you because you deserve to be loved. You and Uncle Ray have given up your lives for Jake and me. You did that, not because of what you got out of it—God knows we both gave you plenty of grief—but you loved us and chose not to be selfish with your lives. You gave up what you could have had for two kids you barely knew."

"But Johnnie, what you don't realize is our lives have been full. We have children, friends, a loving church family, good and meaningful work, and a great community to live in. If we had stayed in Chicago and not come to Cedar Lake, who knows what kind of life we would have had? This one has been blessed."

"Tell Uncle Ray that I love him."

"He knows it, but I'll tell him for you."

"A-Dub, I want to come to Arizona to see Jake. How long are you going to be there?"

"We don't know yet. Jimmy McDowell has been telling us about all of Jake's troubles. We want to talk to Jake and help him figure out the mess he's in with his business. He might need us to stay a while."

"I'm going to call the airline and see when I can get a flight. I'll let you know as soon as I find something. I hope Treeny can break away, too." He winked at Treeny, indicating his invitation to her.

Wilma hung up the phone and relayed the conversation to Ray. "Can we find the chapel here in the hospital? I would like to thank God for what He has done. Jimmy, do you mind if we take a little more time before we go to your house?"

"No ma'am. We can take all the time you like. I want to say my own thanks." Jimmy led them to the chapel. "Jake's been a tough assignment," he chuckled, "and I'm glad to be seeing the light at the end of the tunnel." Flushing, he added, "I don't mean 'the end,' I mean 'the beginning.'"

CHAPTER 14

The 6,000 miles of roads in Navajo Nation were badly in need of repair, even the ones that were paved. The substandard asphalt paving had been a cheap solution to accommodate the nation's slim budget for 2,000 miles of the roads; the remainder were dirt trails. The shifting of the earth's surface had buckled the pavement, creating ridges and waves in the roadway. Riding in Jimmy's double cab pickup truck was bumpy and slow. Wilma and Ray held tightly onto the roof straps to steady themselves.

"Sorry about the speed, but these roads could use some help and it's gotten the best of my suspension," Jimmy apologized. "They both need to be looked after."

"They *are* in poor condition," agreed Ray.

"Yep," said Jimmy. "Neglected like all of Navajo Nation. And this ungodly heat burns up all hope. Just look at that." Jimmy pointed to a torn, faded, decades-old billboard touting a campaign to save young people from drug and alcohol abuse. "They don't have anything to live for."

"Sad," said Ray.

Wilma peered into the distance landscape. "Hey, Jimmy," she said. "What's over there?"

Jimmy steered his truck onto the shoulder of the road and stopped. "That's what I wanted to show you but I'm glad you saw it before I said anything. Let's get out for a minute."

Ray and Wilma looked at each other, shrugged, and eased themselves out of the pickup. They scanned the flat, barren countryside and let their eyes rest on the magnificent rock formations in the distance that had prompted Wilma's curiosity.

Jimmy pointed at the formations. "Look to where the earth meets sky and tell me what you see." They looked past the miles of rough desert to the stark stony rocks, wavering mirage-like in the midday heat. Jimmy retrieved a pair of binoculars from the truck and handed them to Ray.

Ray peered through the binoculars and gave a low whistle. "Well, what do you make of that? Looks like ruins of an ancient city to me. What do you see, Wilma?" he asked, handing her the binoculars.

"Huge columns, like maybe it was an entrance to an ancient city. And a crumbling wall, like it was built around the city. What is it, Jimmy?"

Jimmy took a deep breath, and exhaled slowly. "That's what most people see, but it's not what Jake sees. In his mind, he sees a future city, not an ancient city. He sees those rocks not as crumbling walls but walls that are being built. I've stood here many times with Jake and we've discussed the city he sees in his mind's eye. That is, when he was sober and sensitive to the world around him." He glanced at Wilma. "Sorry, I didn't mean any disrespect."

"Oh, I know you're probably right," said Wilma as she continued looking through the binoculars.

"You know, he really is smart," Jimmy replied "He talks about an idea that would rescue our country from its financial dependence on other nations and it has to do with interdependent communities. His ideas really make a lot of sense, but he always gets discouraged because he says this is too big of an idea. Then he gets drunk, like that's the answer."

"Do you mean that Jake wants to build a city over there?" questioned Ray.

"Yeah . . . yeah he does. But for now, he is only building it in his mind. The Black Mesa—that's the name of that rock formation—has inspired him because those rocks do look like a city. As a Navajo, he is in touch with the land. He believes the land speaks to him and he believes this is a vision of a future city. He doesn't worship Mother Earth, though, like most Navajos. He recognizes God's power and believes the earth responds to God's commands, not the other way around. He loves the land and believes God has given us all the resources we need, if we will only be wise about how we use them. He has talked about a self-sustaining city that could be built because of all the natural resources here in Navajo Nation. A lot of his ideas have come from Cedar Lake. It left a definite impression on him. He's made a lot of comments on Cedar Lake's ability to care for the needs of its citizens. He calls it a micro-economy because its citizens buy from each other and support each other. He says they have sustained a local economy that has not depended upon the global economy."

"Cedar Lake is unique, Jimmy," said Wilma, "and you're right—the locals provide for the needs of its citizens through many small businesses. When the national economy failed, the citizens of Cedar Lake still had jobs and its economy continued to be strong. It gives people a sense of purpose and pride to know their community depends on them. Funny, though, I didn't think Jake thought much about Cedar Lake anymore." Wilma was quiet for a moment. "But he's right. Cedar Lake has survived the economic revolution because its citizens are resourceful and take care of each other. We have also been fortunate that our company, Bledshaw Corn Products and Industries, has continued to prosper in our town. I believe it is because we persistently look for new markets to distribute our products. When one market dried up, we looked for another that needed what we sold . . . and somebody will always need what we sell. It's unbelievable how many uses there are for corn."

Ray agreed with Wilma, "Yep, corn is used worldwide. Charles McGafrey, a friend of ours from Cedar Lake, has been experimenting with using corn shocks in building products. He says you can make insulation and even flooring with the stuff. And his wife says the corn silks can be used to create a new kind of fabric that might be used for everything from clothing to upholstery. They're an innovative team."

"Corn is sacred to the Navajos," said Jimmy. "It is included in their legends and ceremonies. It's a staple in their diets and they believe it is one of the most valuable provisions from God. Jake knows of the abundant uses for corn and realizes what the Navajos have known for centuries: it *is* a gift from God and that it can be grown successfully on this land despite the low amount of rainfall each year. I can tell you this, his dreams about this city include the fact that growing corn will sustain it in a world economy. The by-product he is most interested in is the fuel source available from corn. He says fuel could be the main bargaining product that this city would produce, because of the international mandates regulating the purchase of corn fuel for commercial engines. Many of its other uses would be for maintaining life for its citizens. I'm amazed at his insight in connecting the Navajo culture with the needs of this country."

"Jimmy, this land seems so desolate and has such a feeling of hopelessness," commented Wilma. "How could the people here be revived to take an interest in such a thing?"

"That's what Jake is concerned about, too. You may not know this, but when Jake first came to live here, he had noble ideals about his convenience store. He believed that it could provide the Navajos things to help improve their lives. But Gravél, his manager and partner, played to his weakness. Gravél is not his friend. Jake may have his problems, but he still has a lot of wisdom and compassion. Or at least, God has allowed me to see the possibilities He has in store for Jake."

Ray put his hand on Jimmy's shoulder. "We know the good in Jake, too. That's why we have stuck with him through thick and thin. We believe that God has something significant for Jake to do and we have been praying that Jake will realize it. All those years of being in the limelight with football was greatness trying to find its way out. Jake misunderstood it and took it for himself."

"Jimmy," said Wilma, "you are proof to me that God's plan for Jake is still on track. You have been his angel. You have protected him and believed in him."

"I truly love the guy," Jimmy replied. "At least most of the time," he added, chuckling. "He's like a brother to me. I know he's taken me for granted but I also know the alcohol has affected his way of thinking. Once that's out of the way, he'll be a different person."

The three of them stood silently processing their thoughts and whispering hopeful prayers. Within minutes, the midday Arizona summer sun was scorching their skin, bringing them back to the present. Jimmy broke the silence, "We'd better get going. There's a little girl waiting to meet her wonderful grandparents."

They returned to the truck. "We don't have far to go," said Jimmy as he eased back onto roughly paved road. "I don't know if these roads will ever be fixed. There are many rumors about the corruption in the Tribal Council that governs the reservation, rumors about how they spend the federal monies given to the Navajo Nation for various projects. I could go on and on about the state of affairs here on the reservation, but it might bore you."

"Might as well talk about something, Jimmy," said Ray. "It does look very poor here. In Chinle, I noticed the Navajo people are always looking down, kinda like they're depressed."

"It's considered impolite to make eye contact so they just look down. They're taught not to be forward with strangers, talk too much or too loud," said Jimmy. "It's even important how you shake their hand. A light touch is preferred. A firm grip means you're too aggressive."

"The living conditions seem to be meager and the towns we saw don't look very prosperous either. Did we do this to them, Jimmy? I mean, when they were forced to live on reservations?"

"That's a debatable subject, but in the ten years I've been here, very little has changed. This is how I see it. Modern conveniences have been a detriment to the traditional Navajo way of life and have taken away their purpose. Their culture and their ways were to roam an expanse free of borders, living off the land. They filled their days providing for themselves with food, clothing, and shelter. When they were confined to a specific plot of land, the U.S. government promised to take care of their needs. What the government didn't realize was that their culture, traditions, and religion all revolve around them providing for their own daily needs. They have never been able to transition into modern society because they'd have to abandon the core values of their Nation. And that would mean they would cease to exist as a people. They are proud, and they are trying desperately to keep their heritage alive. Here they exist as a nation within a nation and try, as best as they can, to hold on to their traditions with the limitations and restrictions that have been placed on them."

"What's that mean, Jimmy," Wilma asked. "'A nation within a nation?'"

"They have their own laws and the freedom to operate how they see fit. They govern themselves. The U.S. government has given each Native American Indian tribe a plot of land. That's what the reservations are. The federal government helps them financially in many ways. It's like foreign aid to a foreign country, except that country is within U.S. borders."

"I've never thought about it like that," said Wilma. "I guess I'm like most people who think our government has done them an injustice."

"That may have been true in the beginning, but I believe it's just the opposite," said Jimmy. "I think the U.S. government acted on what they believed was fair, but they failed to understand the traditions of the people. Progress and population growth have created this dilemma. Every society goes through changes that require them to adapt. The choice is to either change or become extinct. The challenge seems to be how to change but continue to keep the values and traditions that make a society strong. Some of the Indian tribes have begun to change, but I'm afraid the Navajos may be on the verge of extinction. The young people know that the world outside the reservation offers a lot more than they have here and a lot of them are leaving to experience a modern life. Those who stay here face the challenges of having no job and no purpose. You know, the unemployment rate here is 67 percent. Since there is nothing to do, the young people are bored and turn to alcohol and drugs for excitement. The Tribal Council and the churches on the reservation encourage them not to use the stuff, but don't give them an alternative. And that would be providing a reason to get up in the morning. Economic development is badly needed here."

They turned off the main road and began a long climb upward on a rough dirt road. Jimmy dodged holes the size of his tires as the truck crawled up the hill in low gear. "I live on top of a mountain. Closer to God up here," he smiled. "And a little further from the troubles in the world."

Wilma said," There is a scripture from the Bible that says people perish without a vision or purpose. I see how that is true here on the reservation. There's nothing for the people to work toward. The government has actually done them a disservice. I can see how that causes debate . . ."

She stopped short of finishing her thoughts. "Ray," she gasped, "you don't suppose . . . Could this be the same plan our government has for the Christians on The New World? Could it be the same as it was for the Indians who were interfering with progress as America expanded west? Relocation . . . ?"

She stopped abruptly in mid-sentence as Jimmy's house came into full view. Standing before them was a barefoot little girl in a white sundress, waving. The wind stirred her dark curls taking Wilma's thoughts captive.

"Oh, Jimmy. Is that her? I think I see a halo," oozed Wilma promptly forgetting her contemplations about relocation.

"Yep, that's Christina. I like to tease her and call her Christmas 'cause she makes most everyone as happy as Christmas."

"I think I'm in love with her already," said Wilma as Ray opened the door to let her out of the truck.

Christina ran to Jimmy and hugged one of his huge legs.

"Hey, baby girl, this is your grandma and grandpa."

She turned to them and curtsied, "Pleased to meet you."

Ray followed her cue and bowed, saying, "Well, we are pleased to meet you, too."

Wilma smiled from ear to ear and said, "How do you do, young lady?"

Jimmy told Christina, "Let's go inside and introduce them to the others."

The house was a simple tan adobe structure adored with pine logs above the windows and doors. Colorful stripped curtains hung in the windows and a wreath made of sage brush hung on the hand hewn wooden door painted bright blue. On either side of the front door were flower beds lined with fist size white painted rocks. Plastic yellow, orange and red flowers poked into the dirt sufficed for the real thing in the arid desert and gave the home a well-tended appearance.

Once inside, the aroma of home cooking greeted them and the sound of laughing children announced this was a happy home. Luisa, Jimmy's wife, welcomed Wilma and Ray. They were instantly at ease in this place. Luisa was a petite but sturdy dark-skinned woman with long black hair and captivating eyes. She had created a comfortable, friendly home in the tradition of her Navajo heritage.

Sometime in the mid-afternoon, Ray phoned the hospital to check on Jake's condition. The nurse told him that Jake's vital signs continued to be holding steady and he was sleeping well. She advised them to wait until the next day to return. She assured them that uninterrupted sleep was a part of the healing process and that the hospital could take care of all of his needs. They agreed to visit Jake the following day.

John called Ray to confirm that he would be at the hospital by the next day, and surprised Ray and Wilma by saying that Treeny was coming with him. John had called from the airport in Denver during a layover before they arrived in Albuquerque late that evening. They would stay in Albuquerque that night and start early the next morning on the four-hour drive to Chinle. They all agreed to meet at the hospital around noon.

CHAPTER 15

They settled in to the warm, homey environment of Jimmy and Luisa's home and the previous seventy-two tumultuous hours melted away. They enjoyed a no-fuss traditional Navajo dinner of mutton, hominy, and fry bread. After dinner, Luisa organized the cleanup and the children cleared the table. Then the younger children brought their colored pictures to show Wilma and Ray and the older ones brought crafts made from native wood, rock and dried flowers. Wilma and Ray gave admiring praise to the children for their accomplishments. At 9:00, Jimmy and Luisa excused themselves to get the children to bed.

"Why don't you two go sit out back and watch the sky? Shooting stars are at their peak this month and you can see a million of 'em in this big sky. We'll join you in a little bit," said Jimmy.

Wilma had been preoccupied during dinner, so Ray was glad when they were alone and he had the chance to ask her about it. "I can always tell when you're stewin' over something, hon. What's on your mind?"

"It's been some week, Ray. We started out simple folks and turned into millionaires overnight. If that wasn't enough to deal with, we almost lost one of our sons, and then suddenly both of them have life-changing dreams. It's an awful lot to process."

"You're right. It's a lot." Ray gazed into the dark sky, waiting for Wilma to talk out her feelings. He hoped she would take the opportunity before Jimmy and Luisa joined them.

"I'm having second thoughts about The New World, and it's not because of the money. I really didn't feel it until this afternoon when Jimmy was talking about the extinction of races. Then it hit me: maybe Christians are becoming extinct. More and more people believe only in themselves. And living for themselves, not helping each other."

"Yep, I agree that people are not trusting in God as much as they used to, and are trusting in themselves more. But Christians won't ever be extinct, and you know that. God's message of hope will continue in every generation and goodness will overcome evil. We know from the Bible that Jesus' second coming will be at a time when evil is so strong in the earth that it doesn't look like there's any hope. We're closer to that than we've ever seen in our lifetime."

"Oh, I know, Ray. I'm feeling a lot of emotions and just trying to sort it all out. And we're living in the 'right now,' not the 'when.' What path do you think God wants us to take? Should we stay here on Earth or should we go to The New World—or should I say, 'The Kingdom of Heaven?'" Wilma said, smiling.

"God is with us either way. We have pursued His ways in everything we have done. Whether we are here or there, we will continue to make God's ways our ways. We have taken the time and effort to know Him. And we have studied to know what being a Christian is about and put those things into practice in our everyday lives. Sometimes it's hard to do, but we have made that our goal. So, we have to ask ourselves: 'Under our current circumstances, what would Love have us do?'"

Wilma fidgeted in her chair and turned towards him. "Can I just say it, Ray?"

Wilma had favorite Bible verses she often quoted from memory. "Sure, hon. I never get tired of hearing them."

Wilma closed her eyes and recited:

> *"Love never gives up,*
> *Love cares more for others than for self.*
> *Love doesn't want what it doesn't have.*

Love doesn't strut.
Doesn't have a swelled head,
Doesn't force itself on others,
Isn't always 'me first,'
Doesn't fly off the handle,
Doesn't keep score of the sins of others,
Doesn't revel when others grovel,
Takes pleasure in the flowering of truth,
Puts up with anything,
Trusts God always,
Always looks for the best,
Never looks back,
But keeps going to the end.
Love never dies . . .

"We don't yet see things clearly. We're squinting in a fog, peering through a mist. But it won't be long before the weather clears and the sun shines bright! We'll see it all then, see it all as clearly as God sees us, knowing Him directly as he know us!

"But for right now, until that completeness, we have three things to do to lead us toward that consummation: Trust steadily in God, hope unswervingly, love extravagantly. And the best of the three is love."

"So where can we love the most? That's really the question, Wilma."

Immediately a shooting star crossed the sky from east to west, followed by two smaller streaks falling north to south, almost crisscrossing, as if God Himself had joined the conversation.

"Oh, Ray, how beautiful! It feels like we're on top of the world." She gazed across the night lit landscape trying to discern where earth met sky.

Jimmy interrupted as he whispered, "You two having a nice time out here?" He and Luisa joined them. "We brought you some chamomile tea. It's Luisa's prescription for a good night of sleep. Figured you could use one after what you've been through.

I'm glad Jake is resting well so you can get a fresh start in the morning."

"The nurse put our minds at ease about Jake when I talked to her this afternoon," said Ray. "I feel a little guilty that we're not there now, but all we could do is watch him sleep. Anyway, we need some sleep ourselves."

The four sat in the comfortable deck chairs and sipped their warm tea, sweetened with a touch of honey. The night was quiet except for the occasional low, distant howl of a coyote. No one felt the need for conversation. In this moment, all was well.

*   *   *

Wilma knew time would not stand still. But if it could, Wilma thought, this was the perfect moment. She calmed her body and emotions as she relaxed. The air temperature was just right, soothing her brow. Her mind scrolled back over the past ninety-six hours, then further back to a time when the boys were children. She remembered how overwhelmed she had felt when her sister died. In the midst of her pain, however, God provided an anchor for her as they moved to Cedar Lake and assumed responsibility for the boys. She recalled how her heart was healed over the loss of her sister and her own infertility as she focused on the boys. She continued to love her sister by caring for them. A lesson she took with her throughout life was that God always provides us an opportunity to show his love. She recognized at times she turned inward by concerning herself with only her own thoughts and emotions; that's when she felt helpless and depressed. But when she reached out to show God's love to others who had needs, she felt happy and fulfilled, and her pain faded into the distance.

She began to consider the opportunity God was giving her right now. The New World would be a nice place, promising safety, security, and purpose . . . free of many of the troubles suffered on Earth. She knew many Christians were weary of fighting the battle against the evil that was expanding its reign throughout the earth. Many were looking forward to the rescue promised by this New World. She admitted to herself that it sounded appealing, but she had a nagging feeling that she still had a purpose here on Earth. *And now this money, God. What should we do?*

*   *   *

Ray's words split the silence, interrupting Wilma's thoughts. "Why have you stayed here, Jimmy?"

He smiled, looking at Luisa. "Well, I met Luisa and this is her home. I fell in love—and love must have its way. On a bigger scale, though, I fell in love with the Navajos. I—I mean *we*—felt by staying on the reservation, we could help these people and make a difference in their lives. We didn't have grand ideas of revival for the whole nation of Navajos, but we've tried helping one at a time. God loves us individually, and we have done that with the ones He has shown us to love over the years." Jimmy hesitated before he added, "There have been three, and Jake is number four."

"You mean to tell me you have lived here ten years and there have only been three people that you have helped?" Wilma blurted but quickly realized her curtness, adding, "I'm sorry. That didn't come out right. What I meant was only three people have responded to your efforts to help and care for them?"

"Oh, that's okay Wilma. I suppose that's one way of looking at things but we've chosen to see it differently." He smiled at Luisa as he continued. "There have been three . . . and not one has turned back to the life they lived before Christ revealed Himself to them. I believe that's remarkable. And the three, well, they have gone on to lead incredible lives, passing on God's love to all they meet and having a positive influence. You see, Wilma, we don't consider changing an occasional tire as help, even though things like that are nice gestures. We commit ourselves to being guardians over the ones that God leads us to help. Just like Jake. He's taken the longest to respond to God's love, though."

They sipped their chamomile tea as weariness settled on them. Jimmy continued. "When I was a teenager I came here on a couple of mission trips. I'll admit, it is a dreary place, but we don't choose what God lays on our hearts. We only choose whether we will respond to the things He puts there. I chose to come here because I believed God was allowing me to see that these people needed help. Even though there have only been three, it matters. It matters to them, and it matters to all the people they will know in their lifetime. I guess that's enough for me. Besides," Jimmy said as he lightened the mood, "God gave me Luisa and I had to stay here 'cause she wouldn't live anywhere else."

They all had a good laugh before agreeing to turn in for the night. It had been a long, eventful day and they were tired. Luisa walked Ray and Wilma to a small hut in the back yard where Jimmy had previously taken their luggage. It was a hogan, a traditional Navajo structure in which they hold many of their ceremonies. Through the years, the hogan had taken on a variety of uses; most Navajos had them on their properties, though they varied in shape, size, and building materials. To Jimmy and Luisa, it was their guesthouse. As Luisa entered the hogan, she took off her shoes and kneeled to say a blessing for the evening's rest. She turned down the bedding on the pair of twin beds and said goodnight.

"This is so cozy," said Wilma as she came inside the hut. "And I'm exhausted."

"I'm ready for a good night's sleep, too" agreed Ray as he kissed Wilma on the cheek. She kissed him on the forehead and they both fell into bed. They were soon asleep.

A short while later, a hawk perched himself on the window ledge of the hogan and gave a shrill, loud caw, awakening Wilma immediately. The penetrating sound interrupted her dream as if punctuating it with an exclamation. She lay still, struggling to pull the dream into her consciousness.

*   *   *

She was standing in the doorway to Jake's bedroom, silently praying that God would protect him and give guidance for his life. Jake was about fifteen years old. She took a few steps down the hallway, stopped at John's room for a few moments, and prayed for him, too. Her prayers for him were different. She prayed that he would know truth in his lifetime, and that his own goodness would not overshadow what God could do in his life. Then she followed the hallway to her own room. Ray had already retired to the bedroom, but he was not yet asleep. He was on his knees beside the bed, praying in a soft audible whisper. "God, You have a plan for these boys. They have given us a purpose, and because of that, I know You have given them a purpose that is greater than we know. Bless them, give them safety, and put them on the right path. Amen."

*   *   *

Wilma was in a hazy state, fighting between wakefulness and sleep, but sleep quickly won out. She was dreaming again.

She was with a group of people, mostly American Indians. She did not recognize their occupations, but deduced them to be architects and engineers, judging by the setting of the room. Jake, John, and Ray were present. They seemed to be standing in front of some sort of white cardboard model. She gazed at it for some time, and realized it was a city. Though she was present in the room, she was observing the proceedings from above. There was happiness and joy as a Native American man, who appeared to be in charge, shook hands with Jake and John.

*   *   *

Suddenly, the hawk was on the window ledge again and gave the same shrill, loud caw. Awakened by the sound, but still in a sleep fog, she managed to recall the dream, and fixed it in her memory. She fell asleep and began dreaming again.

Fire was everywhere. In a panicked and urgent voice, someone shouted, "Get to the lower level!" There was a flurry of activity as people raced to safety, helping one another as they ran. Explosions occurred about every ten seconds. "We'll be safe if we can get to the lower level!" shouted the man. Wilma was again viewing things from above, but was present in the scene.

*　　*　　*

For the third time, the hawk gave its shrill caw and Wilma awakened. This time, she sat straight up in bed and looked closely at Ray, who was sound asleep. Why hadn't the hawk awakened Ray? And why was she having such strange, vivid dreams? She couldn't discern between reality and dream, so she walked outside the hogan to see if she could spot the annoying hawk. She stood in the dark blue night, squinting to see her surroundings clearly. A canopy of stars lit the landscape. Everything was peaceful. No movement. *Is that you, God? Are you trying to show me something? Help me understand . . .* She waited for Him to speak.

After a long look around, Wilma confirmed within herself that He had heard her. She silently addressed God: "*I feel a drastic change is about to occur. Dreaming is not typical for me, and in other circumstances, I would have just dismissed them. But since Jake and John both had dreams, I believe this is you, God, speaking to them and to me. In the Bible, You led people by dreams. I am humbled that You would direct our future in such a way. I don't know the interpretation of the dreams, but I am confident that You will make things clear to us in time.*" Then she went back in the hogan, crawled into bed, and slept until morning.

CHAPTER 16

During most of the flight from Chicago, John was on his computer phone communicating with the office. Treeny tried to busy herself with magazines, glancing up at John from time to time. Finally, she folded the magazine and let out a purposeful sigh.

"It must be something really important. You are giving *that* a lot of attention today."

"I'm sorry, Treeny. I didn't mean to ignore you, but one thing led to another and there hasn't been a breaking point. I'll turn it off and fill you in."

"I don't know if I want to hear your boring ol' work stuff," teased Treeny, puckering her lips.

"This you will want to know. It's family business and even though I'm sworn to secrecy, you should know about it, and this is as good a time as any to fill you in. I should tell you before we see Jake anyway, because it'll come up and you shouldn't be in the dark."

"Oooh . . . secrets! I *do* want to know."

John hesitated a brief moment, checked to ensure there were not eavesdroppers in the nearby seats, turned his shoulders in her direction, and leaned into her. "A-Dub and the girls have won the lottery," he whispered, intently looking her in the eyes.

"Treeny's eyes widened. How much?"

"Seven hundred ninety-eight million. The biggest in history."

"Oohh," squealed Treeny in a low voice as she silently clapped her hands together. "And they want you to invest it for them?"

"Yep, and that's why I've been on the computer so much today. I'm trying to find the best opportunity for them."

Treeny knew the girls because they were Wilma's best friends. They had prayed for Treeny during her disappointments over miscarriages and had been a support with calls and cards over the years. "It sure does seem strange that they would win?"

"Yep. And they are freaked out about it. They never thought they could actually win—never considered what they would do with the money."

"That doesn't surprise me, Johnnie, but I am surprised they continued to buy those tickets. I thought they would want to go live on The New World. As much as A-Dub loves church, The New World sounds like it might be like church all of the time. But to tell you the truth, I've even thought about living there." She paused a moment. "Don't you ever get tired of it all, Johnnie?"

"Oh yeah, some days are a burden, but I've never viewed The New World like a utopia. There are many unknowns up there. Even though Christian values will guide their decisions, the physiological challenges they face are uncharted. This first manmade planet will have to withstand all the tests of outer space—and we don't know what those are. I think one would have to have a pioneering spirit to go, and I'm not so sure I have that in me. Since A-Dub and Uncle Ray are older and closer to natural death it's easier for them not to be afraid since they believe in eternity. When fear is eliminated, motivators are different."

"So tell me about the money they won. What plans do you have for them?"

"I've been looking into The Bank of the World to invest in," said John. "It's an international financial group established after the Second World War that lends money to developing countries. A-Dub will like their goals because they help reduce worldwide poverty. Even if they decide to go live on The New World, she will know that her money is doing good things here on Earth."

"Can't she take the money with her if they go?" asked Treeny.

"No, I've looked into it and the laws there are different. They seem to fall somewhere between capitalism and socialism. There will be a cap on yearly earnings and cooperative ownership of their homes and communities. But they will be allowed to own a business and participate in private enterprise as long as it meets certain goals, with the welfare of the employees being the business owner's responsibility instead of the government's. They don't plan to build their society based on money like on Earth. They claim that societies based on materialism promote greed; their values are based on promoting good healthy living for all communities. The U.S. government wants all excess money invested in U.S. notes or a new type of bond to help finance the national debt. At least for now. The banks on The New World will be savings and loan banks with loans made to promote community enrichment. It will be such a different concept that I believe it will take some time to unlearn old ways and adapt to the new."

"It sounds kind of altruistic."

"Changes never happen if we don't dare to dream, Treeny. I really hope it is successful. Lord knows, we need something different from the way we have lived here on Earth these past seventy-five years. The financial mess our world is in wouldn't be this bad if everyone had looked out for others, not just for their own interests."

"Yep, you're right," Treeny agreed. "But tell me more about The Bank of the World. Their goal is helping to overcome poverty and that sounds like they have concern for others. How do they do it?"

"I've naively stated their goals, Treeny. They are actually quite complex and it has to do with globalization. That's another conversation, though. The reason I thought of investing A-Dub's millions is the return on the investment. It's really quite good. Not only will her money help do good, it will make her more money. That's something she probably won't need anyway, but that's what I do: make money from money. Besides that, I want to find a worthy cause for her money. Often investors overlook good causes because they are looking for the highest yield in dollars rather than being socially and environmentally responsible. But that has begun to change over the past several years."

John shifted in his seat as he changed the conversation to matters of the heart. "Treeny, those dreams I had last night *have* changed me. I don't know how it happened or if this feeling will last, but I am different today. I *really* am not interested in having more for myself. It almost nauseates me to think of how much we have and I haven't felt like it was enough. When I think about those dreams, it makes me ashamed of myself. They made me realize I've been trying to buy love and admiration from others because I thought Jake got it all when we were growing up. It made me jealous, and I haven't been aware of my motivators. That's what my dreams showed me last night. Selfishness has motivated my behavior and I was trying to fool everyone, even myself. It's as if a curtain was opened to my heart to show me the truth of who I've been. When I dreamed those things, I had a new understanding, like I was standing outside of my body and seeing myself the way God sees me.

"Now that I know these things, I want to change them. I don't have anything to prove anymore. It has caused me to want to do something significant with the rest of my life. I want my life to stand for something so I can leave the earth a better place. I'm not sure what that will be; I only know that I have a different outlook now. Even though I've been going to church all my life, this is the first time God has broken into my world, transcended my mind, revealed my life and my heart to me. I don't know if you can understand what I'm talking about, but somehow I think you do." He reached over and took her hand. With his other hand, he caught a tear that rolled down her cheek.

"Would all passengers please return to their seats. The captain has turned on the 'Fasten Seat Belt' sign. It is 89 degrees in Albuquerque . . ." Treeny was lost in the moment. She had many thoughts to share with John, but they would have to wait—they needed some sleep. Maybe tomorrow, the drive to the hospital in Chinle, would provide that opportunity.

*   *   *

Jimmy and Luisa kept the kids inside playing so Wilma and Ray could sleep in. They emerged from the guesthouse at 9 o'clock.

"I have never slept that late in my life," said Wilma, coming into the house. "That hogan was peaceful and disturbing at the same time."

"What do you mean 'disturbing'?" asked Jimmy.

"I had some crazy dreams *and* I was awakened by a screeching hawk. Three times. I thought hawks would be unusual around here, so the last time I heard it, I went outside the hogan to see it. Didn't see one anywhere."

"According to Indian lore, the hawk is a messenger," Jimmy explained. "There have been red-tailed hawks around here, but they are rare. They are mostly in the southeast part of Arizona where there is more habitation and a food source for them. Occasionally they stray from home, so maybe there was one out there last night."

"What were you dreaming?" asked Luisa.

Jimmy interjected, nodding toward Luisa, "She's a dream teller, something she learned growing up on the reservation. When she became a Christian, she began to use her gift to help people understand what God may be saying to them through their dreams. Just like Joseph!"

"Oh, really? I could use some help figuring this out," said Wilma.

"Let me give it a try," Luisa offered.

"First I dreamed about the boys when they were in high school, then about being in a group of architects and engineers talking about some buildings and then about fire. That one frightened me. I realize that dreams come because of things on our mind, so I understand the first two dreams. I've had Jake and John on my mind, so dreaming about our hopes for their lives is understandable. The second dream, I believe, was because of

Jimmy telling us about the city Jake has envisioned on the Black Mesa. But that third dream about the fires has me baffled. I have no idea where that came from, except maybe from this scorching Arizona heat," she laughed.

"Well . . . it seems pretty clear to me that the hawk is the messenger. I believe the message is that you will build something with your boys. I don't know if it is relationship, or something more like a building. The architects may imply an actual building, but the fires indicate that there will be trouble."

"That's something to think about. I mean the building. I wonder what it could be?" Wilma looked at Ray, searching for a response.

His pragmatic answer threw cold water on the women's conversation. "Strange things do happen, but our interpretation of them depends on our perspective. Anyway, I think we should really get going to the hospital as soon as we can. Jake is probably already awake and I'm anxious to see him. Sorry about interrupting your dream stories but we can continue in the car."

"Oh, that's okay Ray, you're right, Wilma shrugged. "We should get going."

*   *   *

Jake awoke and looked around at his circumstances. He was in a hospital bed with bandages on his head and tubes leading from a drip bag to his arm. He reached his hand to his head and felt something attached to it. He also saw an electrode wired to his chest. A quiet *beep, beep, beep* in steady rhythm was coming from above his head.

"I'm checking out. I've got things that need to be done. Where're my clothes?" Jake was speaking into the air as he began to pull the electrodes from his chest and unhook himself from the monitors.

A nurse passing in the hall heard him and came quickly into his room. "Mr. Minda, slow down, please. You've been through quite an ordeal. The doctor will be in to see you very soon. You can ask him if he will allow you to be released." Another nurse from the nurse's station, alerted by the disconnected monitors, also hurried into the room.

"You'd better not get too hasty," she said as she coaxed him back into bed.

A man quietly walked up behind the nurses and peered over their heads as they attended to Jake. His close presence caused one of them to turn around. Her eyes focused on a shirt button, then followed upward, resting on Norman Lapahie, a man she instantly recognized. Though she had never seen him, his presence confirmed the legend about his 6'8" frame, which he augmented with a five-gallon black cowboy hat.

"You ain't goin' nowhere!" he yelled at Jake, causing the nurses to immediately back away. "You and me got business! I been waitin' for you to come out of that coma." He got right down into Jake's face and grabbed the hospital gown at the neck. He drew back his other fist. "I want what's coming to me! Nobody's seen Gravél or the money. It wasn't supposed to be like this." The nurses scurried into the hall, one on each side of the doorway, listening intently to every word.

Norman Lapahie was a very familiar face to Jake and to most everyone else in Navajo Nation. He was their elected Vice President and was known to consort with disreputable people. He had his nose in a lot of people's business and rumor was that he muscled his way into office with the dirt he had on them. In Jake's case, Norman provided the bootlegged booze sold out the back door of his convenience store, making them partners in crime. Alcohol was against the law in Navajo Nation, but with plenty of time to spare and boredom being the order of the day, the Navajos craved the escape that came with drinking. Jake was simply a businessman providing to the citizens what Norman's goons brought him. Jake was certain he had the upper hand with Norman, since elected officials were expected to follow the laws.

Breaking loose from Norman's grip, Jake managed to speak in a cool, measured voice. "Slow down, Norman. I've been out of it for a few days. Why don't you pull up a chair and fill me in?"

Norman backed off as he shook his head and stomped the floor with his oversized rattlesnake boot. "I've been hot since Sunday night. This deal was supposed to bring us a lotta cash and instead we got nothin.'"

"I know we sold a lot of booze, and we had to have made something from the bets on the fight, even if I did lose," said Jake.

"Like I said, Gravél ain't there. The place is locked down tighter than Fort Knox," said Norman. "You got any idea where he is?"

"What do you mean locked down? Isn't the nanny there with my baby girl?"

"Nobody's there. No customers, no nothing."

"We need to get over there. I gotta find out what's going on, where my girl is. I'm not waiting for the doc. Wait for me down the hall, Norman. I'll just be a minute."

Norman turned to leave and ran headlong into John in the doorway, who quickly apologized, "Excuse me, sir. I was hoping this was Jake Minda's room." Glancing in Jake's direction, he realized he was in the right room.

"Just leaving," Norman said curtly. Norman's large frame blocked the doorway as he looked back at Jake. Shaking a fist at him, he hissed, "I'll catch up to you later," and hurried down the hallway.

As he passed the nurse's station, he winked at one of the nurses who had fully overheard his conversation with Jake.

CHAPTER 17

"I didn't expect to see you, John," said Jake. "What brings you so far from home?"

"You, brother." John was feeling awkward, having interrupted an uncomfortable moment between Jake and Norman Lapahie. "Is it okay if we come in? Treeny is here, too," he said as he stepped aside to allow her into the room. "We flew in yesterday and stayed in Albuquerque last night. Drove here this morning . . . just got here."

Jake liked Treeny; she always provided a good buffer between the brothers. "Hey, Jake. How are you? We've all been so worried that we wanted to come and help you pull through this." She stepped up, pressed her petite frame against his chest, and threw her arms around his waist.

He responded by kissing her on top of her head. "Hey, sweetheart. You are as gorgeous as ever." Jake's mood vacillated between anger and joy: Norman had disappeared down the hall and his favorite sister-in-law had come 1,500 miles to see him.

"Sorry, you two, this is kind of a bad moment for me. I'm surprised to see you and honestly don't know what to say, but I've got an issue at hand that needs immediate attention."

"Uh, sorry Jake. If you need to finish something with that guy, we'll go to the waiting room," said John.

Jake grasped for the hospital bed as dizziness overtook him. He faltered and stumbled backward, falling onto the bed.

"I don't think you'd better go anywhere," said Treeny as she pressed the call button. "It doesn't look like you're up to it."

A nurse immediately came into the room, "Mr. Minda, I think you are overly excited with all this company. You are going to have to take it easy for a few days. You have been through a trauma. Now *please*, wait until the doctor gets here."

Jake sank into the bed and agreed to cooperate as the nurse lifted his feet back onto the bed and secured his pillow behind his head.

"That guy seemed really angry. Is everything okay, Jake?" John probed.

"It's complicated," answered Jake. "He says no one has been at the store, so now I'm wondering what's happened to Christina. I've been out of it for three days and I want to know what's been going on. I left a nanny in charge of Christina and he said they aren't there."

"Can't you call?" questioned Treeny.

"I would if I could, but things are kind of backward here on the reservation. Not many people have phones because the old timers have resisted them. I'll have to drive over there to find out what's going on."

"Let *us* go for you since the nurse thinks you should wait for the doctor," insisted John.

"I'm fine, really I am," said Jake trying to convince himself after his dizzy spell. "I had something happen to me last night that assured me of that."

He hesitated a moment, then decided to try out the new Jake on someone who knew most everything about him anyway. "You know that Christmas story about Scrooge? Well, something like that happened to me—and just like Scrooge, I feel very different today." Jake began to tell his dreams to John and Treeny. As he was finishing, Jimmy, Aunt Wilma and Uncle Ray arrived. There were happy greetings all around and Uncle Ray introduced Jimmy to John and Treeny.

After the formalities were exchanged, an anxious Jake turned to Jimmy and asked, "Do you know where Christina is?"

Jimmy smiled calmly, "She's at our house. After I brought you to the hospital, I went back over to the store to see if things were all right and I found her all alone. I took her home with me and she's been having a great time with our kids."

Jake sighed. "Thanks Jimmy. I owe ya one."

"Just pass it on. Care about somebody else."

Hmmm, thought Jake, *that's what Jimmy has always said as a comeback.* "This time I will, Jimmy, this time I will. You can count on it."

Jake addressed his family. "You all must have thought I was on my deathbed to come all the way out here."

Uncle Ray, as the patriarch, spoke for everyone. "We were told this was very serious. The last time we all gathered in a hospital room you *were* near death. This time you were in a coma and we didn't know if you were coming out of it. But God has granted you another miracle. Now, Jake, I know you don't like 'God talk,' but we thank Him for your recovery. And, since we're all here together, we will celebrate that fact." Uncle Ray went right into a conversation with God as if He were physically present in the room. In turn, everyone expressed his or her thanks to God for delivering Jake from this serious situation. After their prayers were finished, to everyone's surprise, Jake also talked to God.

"God, I am sooo glad to be alive. I know You have allowed me another opportunity in this life. I am ashamed that I have ignored all You have given me. I've been angry and selfish and I don't want to be that man anymore. I have failed everyone, including myself, and especially You. The dreams You gave me last night have shown me that my life has been unproductive. In fact, my choices have nearly destroyed me, and all of my relationships are in jeopardy. I ask forgiveness for the hurts I have caused others through my uncaring attitude. In front of these witnesses, who I expect to hold me accountable, I dedicate myself to Your purpose from this day forward." Jake opened his eyes and saw everyone staring at him.

"What?! Nobody thinks I can change?" Jake was trying to lighten the mood.

They all laughed as they realized their shock was evident to Jake. They chimed in with words of encouragement and affirmation.

When everyone had settled down, John began to explain his dreams and change of heart to them. He chose his words carefully, hoping not to steal the moment from Jake during the explanation of his life-changing evening. He shared how his own selfish ways, even though inward, had affected his actions. During his conversation, he admitted that he was tired of living for himself, too. He said he realized that living to get material things was exhausting—and it wasn't satisfying to him anymore. He had achieved wealth, position, and status, but continued to feel empty. He admitted that getting more and more was an endless sucking hole that kept pulling him inward. He saw others getting and having more than he had, and he patterned his life after theirs. The dreams showed him there was something else to gain in this life.

The conversation, accompanied at times by tears and by laughter, lasted a couple of hours and resulted in a new camaraderie between the brothers. Uncle Ray and Aunt Wilma's thoughts and emotions came gushing out in tears of thankfulness. Treeny spoke very little, but silently thanked God for the miracle of changed lives and a future of significant existence. Jimmy listened as he paced in and out of the room, realizing soon he might be given a new assignment.

The doctor, who had been delayed, finally arrived to sign Jake's release papers. Jake had been so caught up in the conversation that he hadn't even minded the wait. He was anxious to see Christina, but his mind was at ease knowing she was with Luisa and the kids. The doctor asked the family to wait in the lounge at the end of the hall while he had a few words with Jake.

"All of your tests show there is no reason to keep you here, Mr. Minda. We can discharge you with a clear conscience. I've looked at your brain scan from yesterday and it shows no swelling or bleeding. It's highly unusual that you would show absolutely no signs of injury based on the comparison of the brain scan we did when you were admitted. Brain bleeds are not absorbed that quickly, they sometimes take years. So I would like to do another scan in a few weeks. I don't think any immediate follow up will be necessary. Your EKG shows that your heart rhythms are normal, and there is no sign of damage from what appeared to be a heart attack yesterday. This is all very remarkable. There are some things in the medical world that just cannot be explained, and you, my friend, are one of those things. Your other wounds and lacerations are healing just fine." The doctor turned his attention to his clipboard as he scribbled his signature on the release papers.

He continued on a more personal note. "Mr. Minda, your reputation is well known in Navajo Nation. There are men who envy the legend you have become in such a short time. I overheard two men talking at coffee this morning. Seems there are some who want to take over your operation. You should be more careful in the future. You might not be as lucky the next time."

Jake smiled, "Thanks, doc. After what's just happened to me, there might not be much to take over. I'm turning over a new leaf!"

*　*　*

Norman punched a number into his phone and paced until someone answered. "Looks like Minda's in the clear . . . . Yep, outta the coma and about to be released . . . Nope, not yet. We'll have to think of another way to get him out of the way . . . . Yep, Gravél is gone. No worries about that piece of scum."

CHAPTER 18

As the doctor was leaving, a nurse pushed a wheelchair into Jake's hospital room.

"Have a seat, Mr. Minda."

"In that thing? I don't need it," he said.

She smiled and motioned him over to the chair, inviting him to sit. "It's not for you, it's for us. Our liability insurance says we need to deliver you safely outside our premises."

"Well, okay," said Jake as he reluctantly obeyed.

She pushed him to the waiting room where his family and Jimmy were waiting. "Can you believe this," quipped Jake, "making me leave like an invalid? But I guess I should be glad I'm leaving in a chair and not in a box, if you know what I mean."

"We're *all* relieved, Jake," said Aunt Wilma. "Now where are we going from here? Our things are at Jimmy's."

Putting his arm around Treeny, John said, "The two of us can get a room at the Holiday Inn, we'll meet you there."

"Nonsense. I have plenty of room at the Fifty-Six," Jake said. "I kind of overbuilt for a house out here in the dessert. I've got five bedrooms, six bathrooms, and 5,600 square feet. Five, six . . . get it? Nobody's ever there but me. Well, and Christina. And a nanny for the past few months. Besides that, I'll need a ride. My trip here was one way."

"Ray and Wilma can go with me to pick up their things," Jimmy said. "We'll pick up Christina and bring her too. We'll see you there in about an hour."

"Okay," said Jake. "I'll go with John and we'll go by the grocery for some grub—have dinner at my place. Bring Luisa and the kids, too."

"Are you sure you're feeling up to that?" asked Jimmy. "We can come tomorrow."

"I feel fine," Jake insisted. "We'll get some easy stuff from the deli. It'll be nice to have you all in the same place at the same time. All the people I care about."

Jake rode with John and Treeny in the luxury sedan they had rented in Albuquerque. Treeny volunteered to sit in the back, giving the twins the opportunity to catch up on things, but neither knew where to begin. Treeny eased the tense silence by telling Jake about her new line of baby clothes for the spring. Jake showed mild interest, but she sensed he was distracted. After patiently waiting for Treeny to finish, John fired off a direct question.

"What happened here Sunday night, brother?"

Jake shifted in his seat and shook his head as he contemplated how to answer. His typical response would have included a way to justify his actions by shifting the blame on someone else, but this time he was honest.

"I've been involved with selling booze to the Indians and it's against the law here on the reservation. Truth is, I haven't known much of what's been going on in my own operation. I became disinterested, pretending not to care because it got to be too much to stay a step ahead of Gravél and Lapahie, both my partners. I've stayed drunk most of the time. It's kind of contagious here, because there is nothing to do. I let my business partner, Gravél, run the place. He seemed to like what he was doing. But Lapahie said he's not at the store, though, and that has me concerned."

"Was that Lapahie at the hospital?" asked John.

"Yeah. He's another business partner . . . of sorts. He's also the Vice President of the Navajo Nation."

"He looks intimidating. I'll bet people do what he says," laughed John.

"He's a bully and he uses his size as leverage. He's hired people to bring the booze onto the reservation and I sell it out the back door to the Indians. Since he's the Vice President, no one ever bothers us."

"So, that's been the secret to your financial success, brother." John said, more as a statement than a question.

"Afraid so. Seemed like a good idea at the time. These poor people don't have anything else to do, so supplying them with liquor seemed benevolent. At first, that is. Then I started to feel sorry for them. That's when the idea of the fight club popped into my head. You know, add a little excitement around here. Maybe even make a few heroes outta these guys. The fights have gotten quite a reputation; people come from miles away. The betting has been good and we've sold a lot more liquor. But in the light of this day, I have to admit, I am ashamed that I have taken advantage of these people's weaknesses. They are good people, they just don't have anything to do."

John cautiously navigated the bumpy road in silence. His thoughts led him to ponder his own weaknesses. Finally, he spoke, "You know, I've taken advantage of people, too, a different class of people, by using a different scheme. I used their greed instead of any need of theirs to gain large sums of money from dubious investment practices. No one ever questioned me. Maybe we're more alike than we thought."

A conversation began to unwind about the land and its history. Jake told John and Treeny that Navajo Nation about its nation within a nation status, that it operated with its own government and laws within the guidelines of the federal government. He also said the reservation was rich in natural resources, but because their religion compelled them to worship Mother Earth, the Navajos refused to extract those elements. Jake cited the example of a previously successful coal mining operation that shut down several years prior under pressure from many of the old timers who believed the coal was Mother Earth's liver.

He continued with the history lesson: Some big corporations had exploited the land without respect for the people or their traditions, much as the federal government did when it originally banished them to the reservation. As peace-loving people, they acquiesced. Over the years, many of the young people sought a future off the reservation. But, because of the high unemployment in the country many of them returned to live on the land of their ancestors. Churches and organizations had come, wanting to help, but their assistance was limited to rhetoric. Jake believed that even though many of them provided a sense of community and connectedness, they didn't provide a reason for daily living. That lack of purpose had generated a lot of depression.

"That's a bleak picture, Jake," said Treeny. "So you're saying that because there is nothing to do, people drink?"

"Drink and do drugs. The meth usage here is unbelievable. They don't value their lives or feel they contribute anything. Many believe their existence is worthless. Maybe that's why I stayed drunk, too. Making all that money hasn't really mattered, either. It seems like the more I had, the more people wanted to play me, you know, for what they could get from me. High school football was all that I ever really cared about. It made the fans happy and it pleased me that I was making them happy. Those days in Cedar Lake are irreplaceable. Football brought the whole town together, and even though I was the center of attention, that wasn't what I really liked. I liked belonging to a place where you could count on other people. A-Dub and Ray taught us about that and so did all the other friends and neighbors in town. That's why those dreams I had while I was in the hospital were significant. They made me feel like my life isn't over. Maybe I can still do something. You know, maybe my life could still matter . . ."

"That was the message I got from my dreams, too," said John. "I realized my purpose has to be bigger than what I can get out of this life. Jealousy, greed, and anger have motivated me to get things for myself so I would gain recognition. It needs to be about what I can *give* in order to make this a better world. I need to leave a mark, you know, do something important—for the right reasons, not just for myself."

"If you guys would ever get together on something there's no telling where it could lead," said Treeny. The silence took over again.

John's thoughts turned to A-Dub and the lottery winnings. That was the most important matter at hand, now that Jake had recovered from his incident. He was trying to determine how to tell Jake, when Treeny interrupted his thoughts.

"What is that in the distance, Jake?" Treeny was straining to see beyond the dust, weeds, and rocks. The horizon had captured her attention.

"Oh that," he said. "It's the Black Mesa. It captures everyone's attention that passes here."

"It looks like ancient ruins," said Treeny.

"Why don't you pull over for a minute, John," said Jake, "so you can see it, too."

John slowed the car and looked for a place to pull off. The narrow, two-lane rough asphalt road had no shoulder but about 500 feet ahead, he saw a dirt road with an orange metal cattle gate. He pulled onto the road and stopped the car. They emerged from the vehicle just as a cloud of dust caught up to them. They shielded their eyes and waited for the cloud to pass.

"It's hard to believe we are in America," said Treeny. "We have just flown here from Chicago which is modern, hi-tech, and basically a wealthy town. Oh, I know we have the poor areas, but this seems like an underdeveloped country from the last century."

"Things haven't changed much since the 1800s," said Jake. "Oh, there are cars and manufactured homes and even a few phones and computers, but there is no infrastructure necessary for economic activity. No water, no sewers, few roads. So, no growth."

"Why is that?" said John.

"Leadership's vision is stifled because the old timers resist change and insist on preserving their customs. They are content the way things are." Jake pointed to the horizon where the Black Mesa extended in both directions as far as the eye could see. "Look about halfway down where those rocks look like an ancient city."

"Is it an ancient culture?" asked Treeny.

"No, just rocks. But it inspires me . . . inspires vision," replied Jake.

"What vision?" questioned John.

"Every time I pass the Black Mesa, I believe I see a city. Most people see the rock formations along the edge of the mesa and think it looks like an ancient city, but I see it as a future city. I know it sounds crazy, but it calls me—no, not literally—but it calls to me, and I think about how great it would be to establish a viable community here." They stood gazing into the horizon until Jake spoke, "Okay, let's go. I just wanted to show you."

"How much farther to your place, Jake?" asked John.

"Ten or fifteen minutes. We're close."

"I have some big news to tell you and I want to tell you in private, not in front of any strangers, like Jimmy." Taking his attention away from the road and making rare eye contact with Jake, he whispered as if he didn't even want Treeny to hear him. "A-Dub and the girls have hit the lottery. A big one. Biggest in history, making them all multi-millionaires."

"Are you serious? A-Dub a millionaire? I can't imagine that."

"You probably have the same questions I do about this. It really is a dilemma. Everyone thinks that winning the lottery is the answer to everything, but now that it has happened to someone this close to me, I can see why some call it a curse."

"Money can be a curse when you're not responsible with it," Jake sighed. "Look who's talking. I believe that's why a lot of people stay in poverty. It's easier because there aren't any expectations of you. Doing the right thing with money is a huge obligation. That's why I've continued to let you handle mine. But you're around lots of money every day. I'm sure you've seen some people do good things with their money."

Now it was John's turn to sigh. "Money *can* bring out the best in people, but mostly it brings out the worst in them. That famous quote from the Bible, 'the love of money is the root of all evil' has been proven to me many times. I've seen people do just about anything for money. I just didn't realize how I had gotten sucked into loving money."

Jake directed John to turn onto a dirt road, barricaded by a rusted cattle gate, for the final leg of their trip. They stopped in front of the gate, where a large culvert, scantly covered by the rocks and dirt, traversed a dry gully. Jake stepped out of the car to open the gate. Out of the corner of his eye, he caught some movement along the embankment. The afternoon sun was shadowing the gully, so he dismissed the movement as a prairie dog, common to these parts. He got back in the truck, leaving the gate open for Jimmy, and they continued up and around the side of a good-sized hill. Jake glanced back; he had a strange feeling about the motion he had noticed. But he was anxious to get home, so he ignored it.

He directed John to continue up the hill. "Normally, you need a sturdier vehicle to climb this road, but I think this Caddie has the power required. Wait till you see the view from the Fifty-Six. It's worth the effort of getting there."

John stopped the vehicle and turned to face his brother. "Jake, you should know that A-Dub and the girls had decided to go live on The New World before this lottery winning. I'm not sure what they will do now, and neither are they. This has changed things for everyone involved. You should also know that this trip out here has delayed their decision. The money hasn't been claimed yet, but I have paperwork that establishes a trust for the money. We'll have to claim the money when we return. I think this little suspension in making a decision has been good. It will cause everyone to be sure of what they want to do."

As they reached the top of the hill, the Fifty-Six came into view. It was both modern and rugged. Huge wooden beams intersected with metal trusses and large windows made up much of the vertical walls. "Whew," John whistled. "This is gorgeous. I've never seen anything like it."

"I hired a great architect to design it and it took three years to build. It's quite a structure. And I love it. I can't imagine living anywhere else on earth."

CHAPTER 19

Jimmy entered the expansive main level of the Fifty-Six, making a huge commotion as he marshaled a man by the scruff of the neck. "Look what I found hiding out in your culvert," he said, throwing a Native American man onto the ground. The man, disheveled and wearing a filthy denim shirt, winced as Jimmy released him to fall face down onto the cold, stone floor.

Jake eyed him intently as he folded his arms across his chest. "That was quite a kick. You nearly killed me."

"You know this guy?" asked Jimmy.

"Just met him the other night—and I'll never forget his face," answered Jake.

"They made me do it, Mr. Minda," said the man, struggling to get on his feet. Jimmy pressed him to the floor.

"I didn't see anybody force your foot to my head."

"They said they'd hurt my family if I didn't do what they wanted. All I had to do was kick you in the left side of your head."

"*Left* side of the head, huh?" questioned Jake.

The hubbub had aroused curiosity. Uncle Ray, Aunt Wilma, and Treeny came into the foyer from other parts of the house to see what was happening. Jake eyed his strapping rival, now reduced to a weak, groveling captive. Jimmy released the man. He squirmed and knelt before Jake, keeping his head down, eyes toward the floor.

"You can press charges if you want to, Mr. Minda. I deserve it."

"What kind of charges are you thinking?" Jake mused.

"Attempted murder, I guess," replied the man.

"Does that mean the kick to my head really was intended to kill me?" questioned Jake.

"Yes, Mr. Minda," he said slowly. "That was the deal I made with them. I was supposed to get paid a lot of money to make it look like an accident. But that's not all. There's a lot more to this story." The man looked around the room at the others, indicating that further admissions needed to be confidential. The others sensed the need for privacy and exited to the kitchen.

"Go on," said Jake without sympathy as he kept the man in the uncomfortable kneeling position.

"Sorry, Mr. Minda," he said as he stammered. "It's just that I haven't eaten anything in three days and I'm a little light headed."

Jake decided to take full advantage of the man's pitiable condition. This captive was not the same as the vicious opponent who had taken him down a few days ago. "I'll get you something to eat, but first you need to answer a few questions. For starters, tell me your name."

"Vic Dennison."

"Who hired you?"

"Norman Lapahie."

"Norman?" Jake stiffened and clinched his fist. "He's my partner. Why would he want me dead?" Norman's behavior at the hospital had confused Jake, but this infuriated him. He turned away from Vic, walked to an expanse of window overlooking a valley decked with earth statues in the distance, and counted to ten to regain his composure before continuing his questioning. In the past, he had always let his anger win the day, but this time Jake was determined to control it.

Norman Lapahie was a thoroughly unethical man. If one course of action didn't benefit him financially, he would find another way that would. He was invariably driven by selfish ambition. Jake, fully aware of Lapahie's character, had entered into a business partnership with him. Lapahie had ways around the law, and Jake needed his protection. Splitting the profits seemed a reasonable price for such a symbiotic relationship. The arrangement worked out well for both men, at least initially. Gravely's Gulch ran smoothly and very profitably for a couple of years. Everyone seemed happy. The Indians got their booze, Jake and Lapahie made lots of money, and Gravél skimmed off the top while Jake turned his head. Jake knew consorting with unscrupulous partners had its risks, but he believed he could always stay one step ahead of them. He was sure Gravél couldn't steal from anyone else this blatantly and get away with it, and even though he didn't know Lapahie's net worth, Jake believed his own net worth to be more.

It angered Jake that he would be the victim of one of Lapahie's devious schemes. His first instinct—until last night—would have been merciless revenge. But he had just undergone a miraculous heart transplant. Dr. Ruach's words rang in his mind, "Your personality and expression of life are defined by the choices you make with your soul." So, he determined to handle this situation differently.

Jake returned from the window, took a good look at Vic . . . and his heart twinged with compassion. "What's got you so twisted?" he asked.

"Gravél's dead."

Jake's eyes widened. "Dead?" Jake put his hands to his head. "How? Why?" he asked in a shaky voice. Even though Gravél was deceitful, he had been Jake's constant companion the past several years.

"I saw it. The murder . . . and the cover up."

"Murder? What are you talking about? Who did it?"

"I don't know the guy who pulled the trigger, but he got his orders from Lapahie. So did I." Vic began to snivel. "I didn't know it would feel like this."

"Wait a minute," Jake insisted. "Watching someone else commit murder bothers you, yet you were going to kill me?"

"They convinced me that killing you was an act of mercy. They said you were trying to kill yourself with alcohol and reckless living and we might as well help you out. But Gravél—now, that was cold. A shot in the head and boom, his life was over."

"Cold blooded murder? Shot in the head?"

"Yeah. Nobody deserves that. No matter what they done."

Vic's words about Jake's irresponsible life smacked him in the face. He hadn't realized others perceived his wretched ways as a suicide mission. *I'm a new man,* he reminded himself as he determined to deal with his emotions later. "Tell me what happened."

Vic recounted the events leading up to the fight and the promises Lapahie had made about the payoff for taking Jake out. He told how he became suspicious that Gravél was going to run off with the money, so he reported it to Lapahie. They agreed upon a plan to wreck Gravél's truck, take all the money and run Gravél off the reservation. Vic insisted that murder was not included in his plans with Lapahie. He swore he had never seen the police officer who was their accomplice. He described the events he had lived though the past seventy-two hours, including hiding in Jake's culvert until someone arrived. He had not known Jake's fate since the fight, but determined his penance would either be telling the truth to Jake or suffering death in this culvert.

"Tell me, Vic, why did they want to kill me? I've always been agreeable."

"Money. It's always about the money," Vic replied sadly.

"But I've always been willing to share."

"That's just it," Vic commented, reflecting on his own temptations. "When you get greedy you want it all. You don't want to share."

When Vic finished his confessions, Jake took him into the kitchen with the others. "This man needs something to eat and drink. Then we've got a decision to make."

A-Dub and Treeny were in the process of preparing sandwiches for everyone. Jake invited Vic to wash up in the bathroom just behind the kitchen and offered him a clean shirt. While Vic was in the bathroom, Jake slipped a vial of tranquilizer in his drink that he kept on hand at work for uncontrollable drunks. He wanted to be assured Vic wouldn't give them any trouble while he was there. Uncle Ray, John, Jimmy, and Jake excused themselves to the den to discuss their plan of action.

"We have to turn him in," insisted John. "Murder is as serious as it gets."

"There is also conspiracy to murder that implicates the Vice President of our nation," reminded Jake. "You have no idea how this will affect these people. Even though Lapahie is crooked, he has people fooled into thinking of him as a strong leader because of his stature and confident manner. The people have overlooked his ways because most of them are apathetic about politics. That allows him to be in control of what goes on around here."

"He'll go to jail for being the master-mind, and Vic probably will, too," said Jimmy. Looks like he's an accessory to the murder. We're going to have to find out who the trigger man was, too."

"I'm not sure how deep this scheme goes, but I think we need to be careful who we report this to," Jake warned. "Lapahie has his guys on the police force and who knows who is in on this."

Jimmy contributed his opinion, "I think we need to go to the top—you know, the president of Navajo Nation. I believe he is an honest man. From what I've heard, Lapahie has bullied his way around him, practically taking over. You hardly ever hear anything about the president, but from what I do know, he's a good man."

"How do you get to the president?" John questioned. "It's impossible to talk to the President of the United States. How do things work around here?"

"We just call him," said Jake. "There is not as much protocol here. He's more like the mayor of a city. You can't really compare him to the U.S. President. There are around 200,000 people in Navajo Nation and his duties are a lot different from the duties of the U.S president."

"Will the trial be on the reservation or in the U.S.?" asked Ray.

"It will be in Navajo Nation. The U.S. is mainly responsible for helping to care for the land as a sanctuary. The Navajo are responsible for preserving their traditional culture and can do it however they choose. The U.S. government lets them mind their own business around here."

"Obviously Lapahie wasn't minding his own business. It seemed like he was minding yours," observed John.

Wilma stood in the hallway just outside the den, listening to the conversation. Her emotions stirred with enormous compassion for a people long forgotten. Her thoughts took her back to what she knew about the Native Americans Indians when they were rounded up and placed on reservations. She couldn't help but compare The New World colony to their situation. Her thoughts compelled her to contemplate the fate of the Christians as a nation of their own. *Will our destiny be similar to that of the Native American Indians? Will we become disenchanted with The New World, with our purpose of evangelism removed? Will living on our own planet be like living on a reservation? Will we no longer need to "make disciples" as Jesus commanded? So what will become our purpose? Didn't Jesus say that we should be the salt of the earth, which provides flavor and is a preservative? Didn't he also say that we are His light in this world and should be set high on a hill so all can see their way? So does the opportunity of The New World appeal to Christians because we have become weary of the opposition against preserving the culture of God's truth and justice? Does The New World provide a way of escape at the cost of abandoning Earth, God's beautiful creation that He left us in charge of?*

The questions in her mind came in rapid fire succession, and prompted her to consider whether living on The New World should be her choice. Sympathy for the Native Americans pulled her heart toward contemplating a course of action to rescue the lives of an entire nation. She began envisioning a lively community whose people were filled with purpose and concern for one another. Silently she prayed. *Father God, I am old. What good can I do for these people?* Instantly an answer came.

"Wilma, the path you have walked has led you to this place in time. All of your experiences are culminating in a most spectacular finish. I have used many who were much older than you because My passions had become theirs. Youthful passions are immature and focus on self-gratification. The mature become aware of others' needs and less aware of self. The truly mature answer with obedience to Me to effect a change in the world, no matter how big or small it is. You have been destined for this purpose."

Wilma suddenly became aware that the men were ending their chat in the den. She heard them agree that Jake would request a private meeting with the president to discuss Vic Dennison's fate.

Jake was anxious to drive to Gravely's Gulch to check on things and make some decisions about the future of his business. As they left the den, he pulled Jimmy aside to ask about Christina. Luisa had said she was napping when they picked up Ray and Wilma's things and that she would drive her over later. Jake was eager to see her.

Before leaving for the Gulch, he looked in on Vic, who was asleep in a guest room. Jake engaged the electronic system to lock Vic's room to assure the others would be safe while he was gone.

Chapter 20

"It's about fifteen minutes from here," Jake said, grabbing the keys to his Crewmax Tundra. Jimmy swung the rear door open and got in. John hopped in the front seat and strapped in for the ride. The fuel rationing had severely affected the reservation, but most of the Navajos scoffed at the electric automobiles being mandated in the U.S. as their poorly paved roads would tear up the flimsy design in no time. Dinosaurs like Jake's Tundra had lived well beyond their years here on the reservation. Jake navigated the familiar route in silence.

Approaching Gravely's Gulch from the south, he noticed the empty parking lot, an unusual sight, as there were always at least a couple of vehicles there. Since the Gulch had opened three years ago, it had become *the* hangout all hours of the day and night. Turning sharply onto the dirt parking lot, the Tundra kicked up a cloud of dust that flew across the front entrance. Amid the dust, Jake jumped from the vehicle, leaving the driver's door open. He singled out the front entrance key on his key chain as he stepped over the dust-covered gas pump hoses lying camouflaged on the ground. As he approached the front door, he noticed that a window was broken and the door was ajar about two inches. Cautiously, he motioned for John and Jimmy to come, adding a "Shhh!" sign to his lips. He kicked open the entry door, bracing for a confrontation, but found the building vacant and in a mess.

He surveyed the pizza restaurant: furniture was turned over and trash was strewn everywhere. He went into the kitchen and found that the food from the pantry and the freezers had been stolen. He walked through the doublewide entrance to the laundry side and saw that the coin-operated washers and dryers were pried open and all the coins were missing. He walked back to the restaurant, numbly righted a chair and table, and sat down. He rested his elbows on the table and put his head in his hands.

Sighing, he said, "It seems fitting, I suppose, that this should end in such a disgraceful way. I thought I was doing some good here, but now I know it's all been based on selfishness—what I could get by giving them what they wanted. And it looks like they got me in the end . . . all of them . . . even Gravél."

Jimmy walked over to Jake and put his hand on his shoulder. "But you made it, man."

"What do you mean, I made it?" asked Jake.

"You made it to the other side . . . the other side of selfishness. You made the turn while you were in the hospital. This just shows you the reality of what you've been living. That's why it's shocking. God's driving His point home by giving you a visual death to it all."

"Yeah. You're right. This is a fitting end . . . and seeing it this way makes me glad I'm choosing to move on. But, there's a part of me that's sad because I feel compassion for this Navajo Nation."

"You might not be done here," said Jimmy, with a spark of hope.

"What do you mean?"

"Maybe there is a different purpose for Gravely's Gulch." Jimmy's wise words lingered in the air, giving Jake time to consider an alternative path. Many times in the past, Jimmy's questions or statements had caused Jake to take a new direction.

"Hmm . . . maybe there's something to that, Jimmy. But we've got some real problems on our hands for now. There's murder and corruption within our government. How are we going to deal with that? Even though having my business trashed bothers me, I'm more concerned about Lapahie and what's been going on behind my back."

John spoke up. "Can you call the president now and arrange a meeting as soon as possible? Maybe he would meet you tomorrow. I think Vic is out of it for today and you need some rest, too."

Jake went to the office in the back to consult his phone directory. He located the number he needed and dialed. Much to Jake's surprise, Leonard Bodie, President of Navajo Nation, answered his own phone.

"This is Bodie."

"Mr. Bodie, this is Jake Minda."

"Mr. Minda, what can I do for you?" asked Bodie, as he pushed back his office chair from his computer to give the phone call his full attention.

"I have an urgent and sensitive matter that I would personally like to discuss with you."

"I have some time this afternoon. I am in my office until six."

"Could we meet early tomorrow morning . . . away from your office?"

"Well, I suppose I can meet you. I don't have anything pressing me tomorrow morning. What's this about?"

"I'd rather not say anything until we are face to face. Like I said, it's a sensitive matter. By the way, please don't mention this to Lapahie. It involves him."

Bodie sat up straight in his chair, his interest greatly enhanced by Jake's last statement. Lapahie had been a thorn in his side since they had taken their offices. It had been difficult working with a person with whom he shared a sordid past and who had come in second behind him in a popular vote of the presidency. Cooperation was problematic because their respective agendas generally conflicted. It was clear that Lapahie acted out of his own interests and bypassed Bodie's true concern for the Navajo people. But according to law, they were stuck together until the next election. Bodie tolerated Lapahie's selfish attitude, but anxiously looked forward to the time when they didn't have to work together.

"You've got my attention, Mr. Minda. I am interested to hear what you have to say."

They agreed to meet at 9:00 the next morning, and at Jake's suggestion, Mr. Bodie would drive to the Fifty-Six where they could talk privately while Vic remained in hiding. Jake did not want to take responsibility for transporting Vic so he would gladly turn him over to Bodie and his bodyguards. He left his office to report the success of his call to John and Jimmy.

Jimmy was busy hammering a board over the broken window and John was cleaning the place a bit. Jake decided to check on things in the apartments—Gravél's, and the one he had built for Christina and the nanny. Nothing seemed out of place in either apartment, but all of Gravél's personal belongings had been cleared out from his. When the men were satisfied everything was secure, they drove back to the Fifty-Six.

Luisa and the children had arrived to drop off Christina. The women, Uncle Ray, and all the children were on the back deck which overlooked a beautiful valley, studded with grand rock formations. Uncle Ray and a couple of the older children were pretending to fish from the deck. Seated at a patio table, with two of the smaller children playing on the ground near them, were Aunt Wilma and Luisa. John scanned the expanse of the deck for Treeny. She was standing off to one side, holding a little girl who had her legs wrapped around Treeny's waist. They were giggling as Treeny pointed across the desert. To John they looked like a painting and he sighed, wishing it hadn't been so difficult to have children of their own. Jake entered the deck behind John and spotted his little girl. He walked over to them.

"Hi, Christina. Have you been having fun at Uncle Jimmy's?" he asked.

"Yep," she chirped as she buried her head in Treeny's shoulder.

"I'm glad to see you," said Jake awkwardly.

Fatherhood had come as a complete surprise to him. When the courts contacted him, he questioned the wisdom of her mother's will, assigning Christina to him. His lifestyle was not conducive for raising a child but he did the best he could, given his circumstances. The truth was, he didn't know how to relate to a four year old. All of his relationships were with adults. He knew how to provide for her needs but that's as far as it went. Christina clung to Treeny, obviously taken with her new friend, so Jake, relieved to know she was all right, sat down at the table with the others.

Christina saw Jake's bandages, and said, "Ouch, what happened?"

Jake tenderly responded, "It's okay, Honey. I just got into some trouble, but I'm okay."

Uncle Ray joined them, and in his typical style, initiated a much-needed conversation. "I am wondering when we're going to talk about the elephant in the room?" The others' silent expressions questioned him.

"What elephant?" asked Jimmy, who had not been privileged to know of its existence.

"This huge, big thing we keep ignoring. The lottery, the money, the winnings," replied Uncle Ray. "We've got to talk about it so we can make a decision."

Jimmy motioned to Luisa, sensing this was a family matter that did not concern them. He corralled the children, saying, "We better scoot outta here, Luisa. We'll see you all sometime tomorrow. Say goodbye, kids."

"Can I stay here?" asked Christina, who had quickly formed a bond with Treeny.

Jake answered, "Yes, honey. You belong here with us. Say goodbye to the kids. You can see them tomorrow." After they said their goodbyes, Uncle Ray, Aunt Wilma, John, Treeny, and Jake returned to the conversation.

Uncle Ray acted as moderator. "We got a lotta decidin' to do. You boys know that we've been seriously thinking about going to live on The New World, but this lottery thing has us questioning a lot. Since we've been in Navajo Nation, both of us realize how much help is needed here. This is a forgotten part of America. It's old America, rich in resources and plentiful in land. I have a hard time thinking that we have spent the money to build an entire new planet in space, yet there are people living in our very own country who don't even have water or electricity. Seems a little outta whack to me."

His remarks stimulated a conversation about the lack of water and sewage systems in Navajo Nation and their speculation as to why it was so. Jake said there had been ongoing battles over the water rights from the Colorado River in northern Navajo Nation. "Development has stalled because, without a main water supply, there's no way to begin to build the infrastructure," he said. "There hasn't been enough money to develop the public systems or services necessary for economic activity, including power and water supplies, public transportation, roads, and telecommunications. The U.S. government gave financial help to Navajo Nation, but not enough to build the towns and provide jobs."

"So what are we going to do?" asked Uncle Ray, corralling the conversation.

"What can we do?" asked Aunt Wilma.

"You can do plenty," John chimed in. "You've got the wheels turning in my mind, Uncle Ray."

"Like what?" Wilma wanted to know.

"Like . . . use your lottery money to help?" John trailed off as if he were asking permission.

"Whoa," exclaimed Jake. "They've got a lot of moola coming to them, but it's probably only a drop in the bucket for what's needed to do the necessary things here."

"Here's what I'm thinking," John said, and he began to explain a plan he had been formulating to invest the lottery winnings in The Bank of the World. He told the others about the bank's mission to help end worldwide poverty by lending to developing countries. Navajo Nation, being its own nation within U.S. borders, would certainly qualify as an underdeveloped country. "We could use the lottery money to hire an engineering firm to plan a city complete with infrastructure, job opportunities, and economic development, then we could apply for funding from The Bank of the World to build it."

Wilma's mind snapped to the dreams she had the night before. She remembered her prayers for Jake and John when they were teens, considering that this might be the long-awaited answer. She also thought of the dream where she was with the architects and engineers. She wondered if these dreams were preparing her for this plan of John's. She had been overwhelmed about the lottery winnings, even hesitant to claim it. But now she thought a vision this grand would be a worthy cause for investing this money and her time. The thoughts of this adventure excited her more than the thoughts of retiring to The New World. Jake was also processing what John was saying. He knew this would be a monumental undertaking, far beyond the capabilities of the four of them. He thought, *Maybe this is only good for discussion. Maybe this is why it's never been done.* Many times, at the Black Mesa, he had envisioned just such a city. But he never proceeded further than mere dreaming. Now, Jimmy's words from earlier in the day were reverberating through his mind. "... *you might not be done here.*" With A-Dub and Uncle Ray's lottery money and John's savvy investment practices, it was at least worth pursuing the idea a little further.

Uncle Ray, with his characteristic wisdom and faith, began to speak his thoughts aloud. "The Bible tells us that with God, all things are possible. If we have faith the size of a tiny mustard seed, then mountains can be moved. The Bible also says that His ways are higher than our ways. Now that translates to: 'Believe God, put some action behind your believin', and watch what happens.'" His infectious enthusiasm and his simple trust in considering the impossible to be possible inspired the others.

The four of them agreed on their objective: Save Navajo Nation by offering its people a future. Their discussion continued, centering on how to marry inevitable and necessary 21st Century progress with the long-held, irreplaceable traditions that defined the Navajo people.

They discussed how extravagant and unregulated consumption depleted the world's supply of non-renewable fossil fuels. The issue had been a major concern of the U.S. government for many years and was a driving force behind the creation of The New World. John cited recent research on alternative renewable energy sources that he had learned about through his investments.

Jake mentioned studies done at Navajo Nation College some years prior, proving that the reservation was a perfect place to build facilities to produce renewable corn-based fuel. He reminded the group that corn was sacred to the Navajo as a life-sustained gift from God.

John talked about the burgeoning global interest in corn as a renewable resource for everything from fuel to building materials. He said he was aware of a strain of drought- and pest-resistant corn a group of scientists had developed during the first decade of the century.

Wilma expressed her thought that honoring the land and sacred traditions while manufacturing and exporting this fuel source would be a key to acceptance from the Navajo people. Ray reminded them how corn processing had sustained Cedar Lake for three generations and assured them the same thing could happen here.

They also discussed the challenges presented by the arid desert climate, and Jake reported that the college studies had addressed that problem. The Black Mesa sat upon a natural aquifer, an underground water-bearing layer of permeable rock from which water was extracted. In the middle of the previous century, a U.S. coal mining operation used the aquifer for slurry to transport the coal and caused it to dry up. Many of the Navajo and neighboring Hopi Indians saw it as their gods' retribution for selling their sacred water rights to the mining operation. The mining company soon closed, rendering the aquifer adequate only to sustain a few individual wells for the Indians' personal use. Many, however, believed that when the coal mining operation closed, the land healed, and recent studies from the college proved the water in the aquifer had returned. Jake suggested funding studies to verify the aquifer as a main water source, thus bypassing entirely the age-old Colorado River dispute.

They ended the late night conversation agreeing that conditions seemed right for their Navajo Nation project. They would use their portion of the lottery winnings as seed money to assemble a group of dedicated individuals and produce the plan. After that, they hoped The Bank of The World would fund the remainder.

CHAPTER 21

Leonard Bodie arrived at the Fifty-Six a few minutes before 9 a.m. Curiosity had kept him awake most of the night. His nemesis, Norman Lapahie, had manipulated him for years because of a shared sordid past and he hoped this was his day of justification.

Bodie had not always been as squeaky clean as he was now. Early in his political career, he and Lapahie served together on the Budget and Finance Committee. Lapahie was the chairman while Bodie worked under him as an advisor. Both were young and politically ambitious; as a result, they became careless about their responsibilities to the Navajo people. They had illegally—but, they told themselves, "justifiably"—skimmed for their personal use U.S. government monies intended for Navajo Nation improvement projects. Bodie convinced himself that Lapahie was the one committing the crime of embezzlement, while he was merely the beneficiary of the monies. Nevertheless, Bodie's conscience got the best of him, and he began drinking in hopes of ignoring his guilt.

One night, after a drinking binge, Bodie drove his truck off the side of the road. In a stupor, he climbed a pinnacle, intending to take his own life. He believed that an angel, in the form of a man, saved his life—physically and spiritually—that night.

His parents had raised him as a Christian, giving him a foundation with solid values. His maternal grandfather, a Pentecostal preacher who liked to say he received his training "straight from God," was little Bodie's biggest influence. Bodie, of pure Navajo ancestry, knew, valued, and respected the traditions of the Navajo, even while blending them with Christianity, making him unique among his people. However, not unlike other young men, he began to stray from family values, experimenting to come up with his own ways to live his life.

Educated off the reservation, he earned a law degree at Stanford University and chose an eventual career in politics. Right out of law school, he was offered a job with a San Francisco Bay area law firm, where he worked for five years. But he wanted to be a big fish in a little pond, rather than vice versa, so he returned to Navajo Nation and immediately entered the political arena. He and Lapahie struck up a friendship based on their ambitions, each having his own interests in mind. Before long, Bodie was sucked into Lapahie's world of corruption. Though he rationalized that dishonesty for personal gain gave him the privileges he enjoyed, his Christian roots were deep, and he continually struggled to find peace. The inner turmoil took its toll on him. Although he married, had children, and led a superficially normal life, he would often go away for days on end to binge. He tried his best to isolate his family from his world of deception and corruption—at least, until the night of his attempted suicide.

His "angel" intervened on the pinnacle that night and whisked him away to a "sweat lodge," a traditional place for ceremonies of purification. His family was accustomed to his periods of disappearance, so that week was not unusual to them. What *was* unusual was the man who returned home. Soon after, he became more involved with his family and more interested in his career responsibilities. His own importance appeared less significant as he concentrated on making life better for others. He began to read the Bible, stayed home more, and, for a couple of years, met weekly with someone he called "A-Man." His family never questioned who the man was, but unknown to them, he was using his own abbreviation for "Angel Man," the one who saved his life.

He started distancing himself from Lapahie, which caused Lapahie to fear that Bodie might reveal the corruption. But that was never Bodie's intention; he simply chose not to participate any longer. A-Man advised Bodie that God's justice and judgment would always win out. He needed only to have patience. Bodie silently replaced the money that he had illegally used.

Throughout the years Lapahie developed an intimidating demeanor, while staying above suspicion by paying, bribing, or manipulating others to do his dirty work. People learned to fear him as a man who "got things done." That reputation won him the vice Presidency in the popular vote contest. Bodie received a few more votes and was awarded the presidency. That angered Lapahie, and every chance he got, he reminded Bodie of his indiscretions and threatened to reveal his past, thereby keeping Bodie under his control.

Bodie took a deep breath and whispered a prayer as he stood in front of the massive, hand-carved pinion wood doors to Jake's house. Before he could ring the doorbell, the double doors opened.

"Welcome to Jake's home. I am his father, Ray Smith," Ray smiled and extended his hand to greet Bodie.

"Mr. Smith," Bodie responded respectfully, tipping his head as he removed his dignified tan felt cowboy hat.

Ray stepped to the side, allowing Bodie to enter the foyer of the Fifty-Six. Bodie made a full sweep of the large open area, letting his eyes rest on the full wall of windows. Ray looked outside before closing the doors to determine how many others had come with Bodie. He noted the two additional trucks parked in the drive. They both endured an awkward silence before Jake appeared in the foyer.

"Mr. Bodie, thank you for coming all the way out here," he said. "We have a situation that requires utmost discretion and I felt more comfortable meeting you privately. Please come into the den."

The Fifty-Six was a perfect blend of contemporary and traditional, but this room was one hundred percent conventional. Dark paneled walls with built-in bookshelves held accoutrements bespeaking masculine interests. A set-back panel framed a doorway leading to the smoking room; a buffalo head guarded those who entered. A bar made from rough-hewn logs balanced the room and a magnificent chandelier made from antlers took center stage. The finishes in the room were natural and a woodsy, musky smell completed the ambiance.

Jake introduced Bodie to John and the four men settled into the oversized cowhide seating. They dispensed with any small talk. Jake recounted the events of the past week, ending with the discovery of Vic Dennison in the culvert. He stuck to the facts, careful not to interject opinions, and ended with a statement of faith in Bodie's reputation.

"Mr. Bodie, because you are an honest man and this discovery reveals murder and conspiracy at a high level, we believe you know who can be trusted to bring this to justice. We have hopes this can change the course of Navajo Nation," implying his knowledge of Lapahie's stronghold of dishonesty.

Mr. Bodie responded cautiously. "Mr. Minda, I have heard of your business practices over the past several years. If what I hear is true, then you are also guilty of some of the things you are implying about Mr. Lapahie. Why do you want me to believe you?"

Jake shifted in his seat, realizing his widespread reputation had reached the top. His thoughts came like the speed of light, vacillating between defending himself and offering honesty. "You have probably heard the truth. I have not lived as I should have. While I was in the hospital, I had time to think about my life. I realized that I have not tried to benefit anyone but myself and I want to change that. I was drawn to Navajo Nation because of the solitude—and, of course, my roots are here—but I soon discovered that despair is so prevalent here. Rather than putting my efforts into positive action, I thrust my own addiction to alcohol upon the people here. For that I am truly sorry."

He hung his head shamefully as Bodie silently empathized with him. Bodie knew how a man could make a turnaround, and his heart tugged on him to believe Jake. Bodie respectfully responded, "Despite your own alleged illegal activities, Mr.

Minda, you are not the one in question today. Mr. Lapahie has apparently committed a serious crime, and I will honestly do my part in seeing that justice is done. You are right, I know who can be trusted, and the first thing we need to do is make sure our witness is protected. This is not a safe place for him, or for you with him here. As soon as his disappearance is discovered, they will be looking for him. I will call a trusted officer to arrange for a helicopter transport. These lonely roads might be unsafe, you know, leaving him open for an ambush. Is there somewhere I can make a private call?" Jake escorted Mr. Bodie to a balcony off a bedroom and returned to the den.

A discussion was in progress. John was listening to Uncle Ray. "It also makes me question the motive behind our government with The New World. We've been told that our world is overcrowded and we are running out of natural resources, but it's evident God's Earth is abundant and people are resourceful."

Jake jumped right into the conversation. "Yeah, I agree with that. The earth underneath is plentiful but it's just like humans to only see what is on the surface. The top surface of this desert looks barren, but below it's abundant with natural resources. I admire the Navajo's respect for the land, but I do believe God has given us all things for our benefit. For example, the coal that was under the Black Mesa. It was good to use the coal to help supply electricity for the southwestern U.S. and Mexico, but it was man's greed to use it without regard to the traditions of its citizens or the future of Navajo Nation. There was never a consideration that the coal could not be replenished. Now corn, that's another story. It can be grown again and again as long as the soil is taken care of properly. I believe that greed has led to the leanness in our country."

Uncle Ray diverted the conversation as he reminisced. "I am sorry that you boys didn't get to live the best times in this great country like I did. It was pretty wonderful. There was plenty for all. People were honest and hard-working, and they cared about each other. That was when the government legislated according to what was good for the country as a whole, not according to every special interest group. That kind of legislation has fragmented our country. We have had to take into consideration each of their needs, instead of each of them taking into consideration our country's needs. I believe the terrible bombing of the Twin Towers in New York City at the turn of the century was a prophetic sign of the shattering of our country. Death and mourning came to many that day as it demonstrated how the biggest and best could be brought down with one act of terrorism. I believe that event marked the beginning of the judgment this country has experienced due to greed."

"Uncle Ray," said John, "I know what you are saying could be true. We are living in a state of confusion and the voice of Christians continues to protest. Some Christians see the injustices and speak out. Maybe that's what The New World is all about. Maybe just like they removed the Navajos who protested this greed, they want to remove the Christians to a place where they won't interfere with government while making it seem like a utopia. That's what happened to the Native Americans when they were given their reservations. They were causing trouble because their way of life was threatened, but it was seen as hindering progress as the west developed, so the government corralled them onto reservations and promised to take care of them. Just look what's happened."

"Yeah," said Jake. "Maybe they do want the Christians out of the way. But the exponential growth of the human population is a problem that *does* need to be solved. The attempts to limit population by abortion and euthanasia haven't worked, so maybe new planets do need to be developed for the future good of the world. Maybe that is what The New World is all about."

"But why make the Christians the guinea pigs?" interjected John. "So if they don't survive, then an entire culture—whose morals, by the way, are a pain in the butt to this world government idea—will die out, too?"

"Maybe all the Christians won't go to live on The New World like they hope we will," said Jake, including himself.

"Maybe they will mandate that we go. You know, with legislation," returned John.

"You boys are really getting worked up over this," said Uncle Ray. "We better stick to the facts and talk about what we need to do. After our discussion last night, Wilma and I agreed to use our lottery money to help build a community, based on some solid Christian values, here on Navajo Nation. If we went to live on The New World, we wouldn't really have a purpose. We believe we would have a peaceful existence, kinda like retirement, but I am more excited about continuing to work toward something that will benefit others. John, The Bank of the World sounds like the right kind of investment for the lottery winnings, but how's all this actually going to happen?"

"Our first hurdle is to get permission from the Navajo people to come onto the reservation to do this thing," replied John as he directed his next question to Jake. "Will that be tough to do?"

"They have been taken advantage of in the past by outsiders. But don't forget our Navajo heritage. We have family land here. That's how I was able to build this place. The land is passed from generation to generation. The 120-acre family plot won't be enough to build this city, but it's a place to start."

Leonard Bodie hadn't intended to eavesdrop, but the conversation fascinated him and he knew that if he interrupted, it would end. He lingered outside the door to the den, and when he had heard enough to pique his interest, he decided to include himself. Entering the room, he spoke with authority.

"We have a council meeting in six weeks. Will that be enough time to prepare a presentation on this community you envision?"

All three men awkwardly realized they had been overheard and Mr. Bodie's question rendered them momentarily speechless.

Finally John, stammered, "Uh . . . I think so. I mean, if that's an invitation, then we will certainly make it happen."

Mr. Bodie smiled, knowing he had walked in at just the right moment. He communicated with God in his mind. *Timing . . . You have great timing. What are the chances that You would have all of us here together, in agreement about this plan of Yours? And they don't even know the ideas that You have already given me. Lapahie will be out of the way and I know many members of the council have been hoping for this.*

While waiting for the helicopter to arrive, the men discussed their ideas for the city to be built on the Black Mesa which would bring economic development to Navajo Nation. They would plan for a commodity to trade. That would provide jobs for the citizens, which would, in turn, stimulate a support industry for residents. Uncle Ray suggested it might be a solution for the economic devastation the entire country had been experiencing. Rather than centralize things through bigger business and bigger government, perhaps the opportunities should be given to local business and local government. He based his example on Cedar Lake and Corny's Products. The main processing and distribution plant employed 22 percent of the residents, while the other 78 percent provided services to the community, from education to home repair.

Mr. Bodie included another example as he talked about Page, Arizona. It began as a construction town in the 1970s. The Glen Canyon Dam and a power generating station were built in the middle of the desert to meet electricity and irrigation demands throughout the southwest U.S. The town of Page sprang up to accommodate the workers. First, jobs were created. Then, temporary housing was brought in. Added shortly thereafter were roads, permanent housing, schools, churches, a cafeteria to feed the workers, a grocery, and a gas station as the work on the dam progressed. The need for this town's infrastructure stimulated economic growth, which continued long after the dam had been completed.

Bodie concluded, "Those men, acting on their inspiration, put into action an enormous plan and positively affected the lives of millions of people. If you ever visit Page, you will feel the vibrancy that still exists today. I believe that kind of thing can happen here in Navajo Nation. It's been my dream for many years, and now it seems more likely to happen than ever before."

CHAPTER 22

"We'll make sure you have a good lawyer," Mr. Bodie told Vic Dennison as he escorted him to the helicopter that had landed in Jake's front yard. "We appreciate your cooperation and we'll request a change of venue to assure a fair trial. I will personally see that Lapahie gets what he deserves. Navajo Nation needs a fresh start and this could be the beginning."

A Caucasian man dressed in khaki pants and a t-shirt with an official badge fixed to his belt jumped from the open door of the helicopter with a set of handcuffs.

"That won't be necessary," said Mr. Bodie. "But when you get to Gallup, cuff him to you. I don't want any ambushes. Make sure security is tight."

"Sure thing, Mr. Bodie," replied the officer. "We'll take care of it."

As the helicopter lifted off, it stirred a massive cloud of dust from the dry desert ground. Bodie watched and mentally compared the dust to the gossip that would stir when word about Lapahie gets out. He turned to say goodbye to Jake.

"We have a lot to do in the next six weeks, Mr. Minda. Don't concern yourself about permission to build this city in Navajo Nation. That will be my problem. Some of the old timers are sure to give us some grief, but as far as most are concerned, it's time for something like this. With Lapahie out of the way, and I sure hope he is, the council won't be bullied anymore. I'll be in touch soon."

Jake reached out and shook Mr. Bodie's hand.

"We are thankful you want to be involved with this. I look forward to hearing from you soon."

As Mr. Bodie drove away, Jake let out a loud "Yee-haw!" and headed back to the den where he had left John and Uncle Ray. Aunt Wilma and Treeny had joined them, along with Christina. There was excitement in the room as they talked about the next steps to take in the investing and planning. From their conversation, it was clear what each of their roles would be.

Jake would be involved with the search committee for urban planners and would act as the liaison between them and the Navajo Nation Council. John would handle the finances. "We'll want to arrange a meeting with someone from The Bank of the World to discuss the plans for our city." Turning to Aunt Wilma John asked, "Do you think the girls will want to join us in this venture?"

"I've been friends with them for 25 years and I know their favorite everythings, but honestly, I cannot answer that question," already having given it a lot of thought. "I know money can change a person. It can bring out the best or the worst in them. Most of all, it's clear that it challenges a person's character and values. Will they be the same as I have always known them? I don't know. I've calculated that we each will get about $103 million. That's a lot of money."

John confirmed her estimate. "That's close, according to my calculations. So even if you are the only one who decides to let me invest it for you, your portion will be significant. But I want to make sure you understand something. We are talking about two separate things. We will invest your money in The Bank of the World, but we will also request a loan from The Bank of the World to help end this cycle of poverty here on Navajo Nation by building this city of the future. Your investments will give you sizeable earnings, just don't be concerned that this city won't be built because the girls may decide to do other things with their money. And it will be up to The Bank of the World whether they will take the risk. The total lottery winnings would not be enough to build a city like the one we are talking about, anyway. We will need outside investors. I hope it will be The Bank of the World."

"So our investment in The Bank of The World could be kind of like the hundredfold return spoken of in the Bible?" Wilma mused.

"Could be, A-Dub. I don't think it's coincidence. If you had not won the lottery, I would not have investigated The Bank of The World. And if I would not have my attention on The Bank of the World, I would not have thought about their mission. And if I didn't have their mission on my mind, I would not have considered the possibilities of a city on Navajo Nation. *And,* if I had not had those dreams, my heart would not have been in the right place to see the possibilities of all this."

Jake punctuated that statement with a loud "Amen!" then added, "And if I had not gotten in that stupid fight, you all wouldn't be here!" After the laughter subsided, he said, "But I know what you mean, John, about the dreams. The dreams or visions—or whatever I had while I was in the hospital—put my heart in the right place, too. What are the chances of all that happening at the same time? I haven't been this excited about something since I got that football scholarship to Purdue. I feel like a kid again."

"It's no coincidence, boys," said Uncle Ray. "This is God's plan coming together in a miraculous way. You see, He needs people to do His work here on earth. He formed the earth with words, but after He made people, He used them to help create His miracles. Oh, I believe He still intervenes with supernatural events, but the miracle is that humans can interact with God to bring about His will on the Earth. Take your dreams, for example. They were supernatural, but the real miracle is that you boys allowed them to change your hearts. Now you are taking actions to back up that change. You will make the world a better place because your desires have ceased to be selfish."

"Uncle Ray, you have such wisdom," interjected Treeny. "I love it when you give us your insights." She stroked Christina's dark curls as the precious little girl sat on Treeny's lap, playing with a fluffy stuffed bunny.

Wilma stood and walked to the window. "You're right, Ray. God still needs us here on Earth. Even though going to The New World seems so peaceful, I believe God is giving us a choice. I am at peace about our choice to stay and see this city built. I don't know how much I can do, but I can pray. There are so many needs here that it would be wrong to turn our backs when John says we can help. That lottery money seemed like a curse, but now that all of this has happened I believe it is a blessing. The fate of The New World is unknown and so is this city in Navajo Nation. My heart keeps drawing me to stay here." She laughed as she realized, "We all keep talking about our hearts as if that's where decisions are made."

"It isn't where decisions are made, but it is where our nature resides," Uncle Ray responded. "I believe your head is where you make decisions. Your heart can tell you one thing, but your head can cause you to do another. God gave us the ability to have His nature, but it's up to us to choose it. I think our head is our will—you know, the part of us that decides how we're going to act—and we can agree with what God puts on our heart or not."

The room grew quiet as all contemplated Uncle Ray's words. Each was choosing to respond to God's nature within, and to act accordingly. After a few moments, Uncle Ray spoke again, "I want to pray and ask God to guide us as we move forward with this plan." They were reverent as Uncle Ray prayed.

Christina slid from Treeny's lap and onto her knees as she folded her hands together. Treeny was touched as she looked upon this child's innocent faith. Her mind wandered as she imagined Christina in the brilliant blue color for her new line of clothing. *Maybe I can expand my line to include kids' clothing up to size 6. She would look adorable in blue and white against her dark skin and hair.* Treeny was struggling again with her desire to have a child of her own. She was imagining what it would be like if Christina came to live with her and John. They had made an immediate connection, but Jake clearly cared about her and she knew it wouldn't be right to separate them. Jake admittedly needed help with her or he wouldn't have hired a nanny, and Luisa definitely had her hands full. He didn't have anyone reliable to help with her. *Oh, God, please help me with the longings I have to be a mother. I do not want to go through this depression again. She is my niece, not my daughter. I will be a good aunt and plan to visit frequently. Help Jake find someone he can trust to help with Christina.*

She reminded herself of what Uncle Ray had just said: our head is our will, the part of us that decides how we are going to act. She was determining to act as an aunt and not fantasize about being a mother. She mentally rejoined the others and Uncle Ray's prayers.

As the prayer ended, everyone scattered to attend to their own matters. John and Treeny went to their room to decide on air travel plans back to Chicago. Ray and Wilma went to the kitchen to fix lunch for everyone. Jake decided to drive to Gravel's Gulch to plan the cleanup. Christina asked his permission to stay and play with Treeny. He smiled his approval, tousling her hair as he left the house.

As Jake pulled his Tundra out of the garage, a familiar, nagging feeling of loneliness swept over him. It was the first time he was alone since his hospital stay. His normal response to these feelings was a drink—and usually another one, or two, or three . . . *I bet the vandals didn't find the liquor. I'll see if my favorite single barrel whiskey is still in its hiding place.* He bore down on the gas pedal, waging an argument inside himself. *You don't need that anymore. That's how you got in all this trouble, by not dealing with feelings and emotions. Remember when Dad didn't show up to that game in high school when the recruiters were coming? He stood you up even after you went to Sonnies' to give him a personal invitation. You vowed since he wouldn't join you, then you would join him . . . in the bottle. And brother, you have.*

Jake saw a sliver of something dark lying in the road just ahead. As he rapidly approached, he could tell it was a large black snake. Normally he would have swerved to miss it, but his frame of mind at that moment demanded that he crush it. He flattened the snake and drove a little faster, hearing the *thump, thump* under his truck as his tires threw the snake up against the undercarriage. His palms began to sweat as he struggled with his emotions. A battle was taking place inside him as he fought to keep his resolve.

He forced himself to seek the nearest help available so he swung onto a rough dirt road leading to a little rough-hewn chapel on top of a knoll. It was a simple adobe structure with a wooden cross atop the open doorway, and it beckoned him as his only refuge against this wave of temptation. He believed that surrounding himself with God's presence in this tiny chapel would be his fortress. He convinced himself that he needed the reassurance of what this structure stood for. He slammed the truck to a stop, leaped out of the cab, and desperately ran to the altar. Falling to his knees, he cried, "God, HELP ME! I *will* break these destructive habits but I need Your help. I have disappointed You and everyone in my life. That is changing NOW!"

Jake broke into a sweat as he rocked back and forth on his knees. Tears flowed down his face as he bared his soul. All of his past sins rolled through his mind as the accuser attempted to discourage him. "NO! I am not that man anymore," he shouted loudly, his hands over his ears. "I forgive you, Dad, for not loving me like I wanted you to. I forgive you, Mom, for leaving me when I needed you. God, please forgive me . . ." Remembering his dreams, he summed up the words of Dr. Shammah, Dr. Rauch, and Dr. Yeshua. *I will make a choice that lines up with God's Spirit inside of me and we will overcome what this body is screaming for. I choose life, not death.* His body trembled as he cried out to God for deliverance from his torment.

Suddenly and silently, a large warm hand rested gently on his shoulder. He was no longer praying alone. Another voice, one that Jake recognized, was praying also. He had heard Jimmy praying for him many times before, when Jimmy thought he had already passed out from too much drink, but this was the first time they prayed together. Jake's trembling stopped as an all-encompassing calm came over him. After the prayers, both men sat in silence for several minutes as Jake recovered from his emotional ordeal.

"Thanks," said Jake.

"For what?" asked Jimmy.

"For being there for me. For *always* being there for me," replied Jake.

"You were my assignment. That is, until today."

"What do you mean, *assignment*, Jimmy?"

"God assigned me to keep watch over you. About seven years ago. I thought this day would never come."

"What's so special about today?"

"You made it."

"Made what? What are you talking about?" questioned Jake.

"You chose God's plan for your life over what you wanted. You overcame a great temptation in your life that would have kept you derailed, one that you wouldn't have been willing to give up just one short week ago. But most of all, you decided to not let unforgiveness rule your life anymore. You realized what was causing your anger and destructive behavior. You extended forgiveness to your parents, who let you down when you were a kid. The Bible tells us that when we forgive others, God will forgive us. So . . . you made it."

"Whew, that was rough, but I feel peaceful now." Jake wiped the sweat from his forehead with his sleeve and struggled to his feet.

"You did a dangerous thing, my friend. You dedicated your life to God when you came out of that coma. When you do that, a test usually comes next, to see how serious you are. And they weren't just words. You've proven today that you intend to follow through with the commitment you made to God."

"You're right, Jimmy. I can see that it won't be easy. But I am determined that I'm not going to follow the path of least resistance and give into every whim. I want my life to stand for something and I want to be proud of it."

"That's the key, Jake. You ain't livin' for yourself anymore. You're living for others and that is God's way."

Jake let that sink in for a minute before he thought about what Jimmy had said. "Seven years, huh? That's a long time. I guess you could say I owe you my life."

They both had a good laugh before Jimmy gave him a vote of confidence. "Even though you've been a pain in my backside at times, you're worth it."

CHAPTER 23

Ray and Wilma had purchased a one-way plane ticket to Albuquerque, not knowing how long they would be with Jake. But by the end of the week, he was well enough to resume his daily activities, so they decided to return to Cedar Lake. The week had been full of events, with no time to discuss their future. First, the issue about the lottery money had to be decided with the girls. John had discussed good ideas with them, but they knew the others had been making their own plans for their winnings. They also needed to put a timeline to their move to Arizona. To give themselves sufficient time to discuss these matters, Ray and Wilma decided to rent a car and drive back home. Jake drove them to the nearest car rental office, six hours away in Gallup, New Mexico. Goodbyes were short and Ray and Wilma drove off in a luxury car, a rare indulgence, courtesy of the lottery win.

"I'm gonna miss the girls," Wilma said to Ray shortly after they began the long drive home.

"Yeah, me too. It just means you'll have to spend more time with me," teased Ray. "Think you can stand that?"

"Oh, sure," she smiled. "You're the love of my life and I can't think of any one person I'd rather be with. It's just going to be a little quieter."

"That's for sure. I think of you all like a gaggle of geese when you're together," laughed Ray, honking and making hand gestures indicating talking.

"I'm surprised none of them have called me while we've been here. I thought they might have called to check on Jake."

"Well, I didn't see you call any of them, either. Did you?" questioned Ray.

"No, but they are always the ones to call me."

"Come on, Wilma, be honest. This money thing is a disruption in your friendship, isn't it?"

"I don't like to admit it, Ray, but it feels like it might be. Kinda like being way out here in Arizona, it does put distance between us. We've always shared all of our feelings. Why not with this?"

"Have ya now?" probed Ray.

"Well, yeah. What are you implying?"

"I've observed these girls for a long time now. Wilma, it's no secret that you're the hub. Those girls need your approval for everything. You're strong, competent, and opinionated. Maybe, just maybe, winning this money has somehow empowered them to stand on their own two feet."

Wilma was quiet as a red blush of embarrassment crept across her face. "Then I'm glad they won that money. If what you say is true, then maybe it is about time they thought for themselves."

"Just maybe they've been making some decisions they're afraid you won't agree with. I mean, you have always done everything together because your lives have been so similar. This money gives all of you different choices."

"I hope they make wise choices." They drove along without another word as Wilma contemplated what Ray said.

Wilma finally broke the silence. "Ray, how far out of our way would it be to drive to one of the launch sites for The New World?" she asked as her thoughts changed directions.

Ray gave Wilma a surprised look. "Why would you want to go there? I thought our decision was to stay."

"Just curious."

"Do you remember where they are?"

"I know there's one in New Mexico. I heard they needed permission from Navajo Nation to build it."

"A few months ago, the launch sites were secret, but now that it's public knowledge, we can find it easily on the Internet."

Wilma pulled the handheld wireless computer out of her bag and typed in a search for The New World launch locations. Fifty-four websites popped up. She chose the one denoted "Official." Scanning the site's homepage, she noted a location in Burnham, New Mexico. She read the text to Ray.

> Burnham, New Mexico is one of four NASSA official launch sites for The New World. Permanent human occupation of space begins here as volunteer groups are transported to sustain life on this fabricated planet.
>
> Burnham offers dormitory-like accommodations while awaiting launch schedules. A two-week stay is included with passage fees. All meals are served in a cafeteria setting. Auto brokers in the nearby town of Newcomb offer free shuttle services with prior arrangements for auto purchase. Storage of personal belongings must meet regulations.
>
> Citizenship is a requirement for living on The New World. The two-week training, designed to facilitate the transition to The New World, includes _daily seminars,_ held at the Burnham Community Center, to inform new citizens of expectations on The New World. Testing and a swearing-in ceremony conclude the two weeks of preparation for citizenship in this first interplanetary community. Free ongoing education is provided encouraging active citizenship, whereby all citizens are urged to work towards the betterment of their new community through economic participation, volunteer work, public service, and other efforts designed to improve life for all of its citizens.
>
> Open forums are held on the first and third Sunday at 3:00 p.m. in the Burnham Community Center. The two-hour presentation includes a detailed description of The New World, its physical make-up, social

communities and government structure, and a reading
of the New Constitution. <u>Reservations</u> are required, as
seating is limited.

"Let's go to that," offered Wilma.

Ray gently inquired, "Are you questioning our decision to stay and help on Navajo Nation?"

"No, we have made our decision. But I think it would be helpful to know what the plans are for the future of our world, er, I mean, our solar system. This is history in the making. We're so close to Burnham and the seminar is tomorrow. How can we pass this up?"

"You're right, Wilma. It is a great opportunity. Call to see if you can make a reservation and check on a hotel in Newcomb for tonight." Wilma busied herself with the computer while Ray's mind drifted.

*   *   *

How would life be different on a fabricated planet. God's creation was so awesome and diverse, Ray couldn't imagine not dwelling in this earth-temple of God's splendor. He had his doubts prior to their trip to Arizona, but in the midst of the stark beauty of this land, his hope in America was renewed. He compared the bleak state of Navajo Nation to the bleak state of affairs this country had fallen into over the past couple of decades. He believed he had experienced the best times in America and was looking forward to extending hope to others. He had lived in times when there was a 3.4% unemployment rate, when most people had meaningful work and their own homes to live in—along with purpose and satisfying interaction in their social circles.

He also knew that extreme materialism, driven by greed during an age of decadence, had led to overwhelming debt. This ultimately caused an indifferent attitude about ownership of property, which gave way to lack of responsibility born of effortless gain. He had seen the post-industrial age leave entire communities without a reason for existence. Individualism had led to isolation as devotees of online life had built and inhabited their own virtual reality. He had been saddened that self-absorption had overturned good manners and respect for others. In Chicago, he had seen chic dwellings rehabbed from old factories, the only remnants of this past flourishing age. *No wonder The New World and its values seem revolutionary. Most of the people living in post-Christian America don't remember when America was "one nation under God."*

He thought of some things he had read about the 'The New World Declaration of Independence' presented to the U.S. government during the initial committee meetings prior to Senate approval of this new Christian nation. The tenets of the declaration were based on the Ten Commandments; Ray knew all true believers already had those commandments written on their hearts. The paper only existed to confirm those values. Ironically, the idea of Christians becoming their own nation was revolutionary to Ray, too, but in a different way. He remembered when America *was* a Christian nation. No one needed to state it as a fact, it just was. The laws were based on Christian values but over time, tolerance to other philosophies paved the way for an overriding paradigm of equally accepting all views. The U. S. Constitution had become diluted with so many amendments that citizens became confused . . . and then apathetic. Not many of them remembered or cared about America's original ideology, so they blindly accepted the nation's philosophical merger with the international world.

The government steadily asserted control over food, water, energy and fuel supplies, transportation, banks, healthcare, and education. Excessive taxation for these socialistic benefits constrained private industry so that the only ones remaining were smaller firms in craft and specialty fields. No one worried about provision for their daily needs, those had become the government's responsibility and the citizens' right. This "I'm not responsible" attitude led to a drastic increase in brazen crime.

Ray wondered, *Have the people become slaves to the government or has the government become a slave of the people?*

*   *   *

Wilma interrupted his thoughts. "Oooh, Ray. I decided to search a few of these websites and found the personal webpage of Malachi Gentry, who is organizing the Christian volunteers." Wilma turned up the speakers so they could both hear Malachi's message:

> *"The New World is the single most important issue facing Christians today. Our government has given us the opportunity to inhabit the first of many fabricated planets to establish a new nation, a Christian nation. We should feel privileged; instead, many of you are afraid. I know that every Christian is asking himself whether he wants to live on The New World. This question is what we all should ask ourselves every day. Consider that God may take us into His kingdom of heaven at any moment. Consider that The New World represents heaven. Consider that you have time to examine your lives and make a decision about your future.*
>
> *"I urge each of you to look within and ask why you might have fear. Could it be regret, or could it be the love for things you have here? If it's regret, then search what is causing you sorrow. Have any of your past actions caused hurt to others? If so, then it is time to make them right. Or are you holding grudges against others who have wronged you? Then forgive. Go to people and make things right.*
>
> *"Let me ask you about the love of things? If a fire or a flood destroyed what you have, would it destroy you, too? Don't let your identity be in things. Let them be in God and in Godly behavior. Let your inner life be peaceful, not by being satisfied in having or not having things, but*

by having a relationship with God Himself. There is no greater satisfaction in this life, and it is something that cannot be taken.

"Now there is another reason that you may be afraid. This may be the granddaddy of them all. Could you be afraid to give up lordship of your own life, to trust someone other than yourself with answers? Whom do you call 'Lord'? Who is the master and ruler of your life? Who motivates you to action? Have God's ways become your ways? Not yet, you say. Well, are you at least working on it? Jesus Himself taught us how to pray, and He said we should pray that God's will be done on earth as it is in heaven. The trouble is, most of us pray for what we want and ask God to bless it.

The problem most of us have with praying God's will is that it takes faith. Faith believes to the point of letting go of what we know. When we limit our prayers to what we know, we forget that God's wisdom and solutions go beyond our knowledge. He is the Almighty, the Creator of the universe, Maker of humankind. Don't you think He has solutions and answers to life's difficulties that we don't have a clue about? He's smart—really smart. And He is multidimensional. What I mean is that each solution He presents doesn't just solve one problem; it affects many other situations and presents solutions to them as well. WOW! What a God He is!"

Wilma clicked off the speaker. "Ray, I mentally answered Malachi's questions, and under ordinary circumstances I think I would definitely be ready to go to The New World. But something has happened to us in the past week that has caused my thinking to be different."

"Mine too, Wilma. Most of my life I have believed that God would rescue us Christians out of our helpless situations. Eventually that would be heaven, but until then, we were just waiting and doing the best we could. But I've been contemplating the phrase that Jesus used over and over: 'the kingdom of heaven is within.'" I've been thinking that if every believer acts on Godly principles, that is what brings the kingdom of heaven to Earth. I'm beginning to believe that the kingdom of heaven is not only a place in the sky, but also place of shared peace established by believers being who God says they should be."

Wilma quietly considered Ray's words. She, too, had experienced an abrupt shift in her beliefs. The circumstances they found themselves in required them to look at life differently. In Cedar Lake, things had been the same for years, despite global changes. Now, they found themselves unexpectedly placed into this particular situation for reasons beyond their understanding. Their only choice was to act on the values they knew to be right.

Ray broke the silence. "We have been plunged into something extraordinary. Did you ever think we would be the ones who would set the wheels in motion to potentially save an entire nation?"

Wilma looked at him peacefully. "Not in a million years."

CHAPTER 24

The Best Western hotel in Burnham, New Mexico, stood as a gleaming, freshly painted beacon pointing the way toward the future as the last stop on planet Earth for the few and the brave.

Ray and Wilma arrived for check-in a few minutes after four in the afternoon. Monitors in the lobby flashed continual images of The New World beginnings for this people of faith: homes, parks, transportation, greenhouses, and work environments. People watching the video high-fived each other, signifying a triumph of rescue and deliverance from the despotism of a government that seemed bent on destroying the very foundation of its existence. This opportunity renewed their hope in God and the divine destiny they believed in. The assimilated Christians of the secular world were missing in this separatist environment exclusively reserved for those who believed beyond reason and without doubt. Most compared this exodus to that of the Israelites who fled from Egypt in search of the Promised Land. The journey also appealed to those who had nothing to lose and everything to gain.

Upon checking into the room, Wilma expressed her thoughts to Ray as she contemplated the departure of her life in Cedar Lake as the reality of Christians leaving Planet Earth began to sink in. "You know Ray, things will never be the same for us again."

"You're right, Wilma. The past twenty-five or thirty years have been so predictable. Each day rolled out before us with just enough on our plates to keep things from getting boring. I've loved our life."

"Me, too. Things have been peaceful, even though we've known how things are around the world."

"You know it will eventually affect Cedar Lake, too. And probably soon."

"We've had a good life, Ray."

"You know we've been pushed out of our nest."

"Yeah, a big push. That's what it feels like. We've been cozy in our little corner of the world. Now it seems like God is requiring something more from us. But all day I've questioned whether I'm ready. I mean, things are so bleak on the reservation. We've got our home, church, my job, and most of all, my friends. I'll miss them most of all. And besides that, I'm wondering if we're too old for this."

"You changing your mind?" he asked.

"Cold feet, I suppose."

"Why don't you call the girls? Maybe talking things over with them will help. I'll go to the lobby to see where we can get some dinner."

As the door shut behind Ray, Wilma sat on the bed with her phone. She dialed Suzi's number, mentally replaying a recent conflict she had had with Suzi.

*   *   *

Wilma was pacing the floor in her kitchen. It was 10:00 p.m. on a Friday night; she had left the church two hours ago. She and Suzi had had another confrontation. This time it was about the color of the napkins for the Mother's Day Tea. How stupid. Who really cares whether they are lavender or pale blue? Why do we always debate about the silliest things? We should just get white ones and get over it.

Deep in her thoughts, she was startled by the phone ringing. "Hi, it's Suzi. You mad at me?" she asked in a pouty voice.

"Nooo. I just don't know why we always have to do this."

"'Cause I got opinions too, Wilma. You get what you want a lot."

It's napkins, for heaven's sake, Suzi. Get over it, Wilma thought to herself. "So we'll get the pale blue instead of the lavender if it's that important to you."

"It's not the napkins, Wilma. I just don't like arguing with you, especially over something this ridiculous. I just wish for once that you would want what I want. That's all."

"So we'll get white ones!" Wilma shouted. They both burst into hysterical laughter that led to tears.

"I'm sorry," said Wilma.

"Me, too," said Suzi. "So, we'll get white ones and dare anyone to notice."

The Mother's Day Tea came and went while the white napkins, deposited in the trashcans, proved once again to Suzi that her simple desires went unmet.

*   *   *

"Wilma, is that you?" asked Suzi, reading the caller recognition feature on her phone.

"Yeah, Suzi. It is me. How's everything going"?

"It's good. Yeah, real good. Yeah, no, I'm lying. I'm a mess. I can't believe you had to leave town so soon after our big news. It's been hard not to say anything. But I think it slipped out because people are beginning to ask questions. But I didn't say anything, except to my daughter-in-law. Had to tell her, but made her promise not to say anything. I've been staying home so I didn't have to see anybody. Even missed work last week." Suzi spouted her broken sentences without a break.

"Hey, girl. Slow down a minute. You don't sound okay. What's going on?"

"Whew . . . I feel like I'm losing my mind. I went to the graveyard to talk to Jim about things, 'cause I knew it wouldn't matter if I talked to him. He sure wasn't going to spread it around."

"Didn't you talk to Margaret or Barbra Jean?"

"No. They packed up and went to the beach for the week with their families."

"What about Jean? Have you talked to her?"

"She's been in the hospital with her heart again. I don't think she can take all of this. She's been in critical care. Pastor Charles said they want to do a transplant this time."

Wilma suddenly realized the impact of having left Cedar Lake at such a critical time. She knew her friends relied on her to make things go smoothly. This time, however, they were left to make decisions as individuals, not as a group, and this was the most important decision they had ever faced. She had known their weaknesses, but until now she hadn't considered how those weaknesses would be exposed in the light of winning this money. This filled her with an unexpected concern.

"Suzie, what's happening to us?"

"It's the money, Wilma. I think it's a curse. You know what I've been doing this week while I've been home? Watching the home shopping channels and ordering things I don't even need. I'm so ashamed of myself. I feel like I'm finally getting to do what I want to do, and it feels really good. But later when I try to sleep, I'm haunted by guilt. I love it and I hate it at the same time." Suzi started to cry.

Wilma's compassion kicked in. "Suzi, it's okay. Maybe you deserve a little spending spree. What girl doesn't enjoy the pleasure from getting something new?"

Suzi blurted out between sobs, "But Wilma, I ordered a garden tiller! What am I going to do with that?"

"Maybe you were thinking of the man next door who is always kind enough to do your trimming. It would make a nice gift."

"Oh, Wilma," her sobs turning to a wail, "what is the matter with me? I even ordered five designer handbags. The same bag in five colors because I couldn't make up my mind. And just because I knew I could."

All of Wilma's efforts to comfort Suzi were of no avail. It was obvious that Suzi's suppressed feelings had surfaced like a whale, blowing to high heaven. Wilma had been aware of those negative feelings in the past, and the group always tried to tiptoe around them. Sometimes the group resented her ability to manipulate the circumstances to go her way, but in the end, they gave in to her emotional needs. After all, she had lost her husband and her only son in the same car wreck. Wilma continued to listen to Suzi's babblings until she calmed herself.

"So, that's it, Wilma. I am losing my mind over this lottery. I don't know who I am anymore. Knowing I have this money changes everything about me," she confessed.

"The money doesn't change you, Suzi, but the way you think about the money can change you. You can choose."

"But I don't think I want to be me anymore. I can be someone else now. I haven't been happy since Jim and Aubrey died. I think I died then, too. Nothing has made me happy since. This money gives me the opportunity for happiness again."

"Suzi, money can't bring them back, nor can it buy you happiness."

"Well, I think I'm going to try."

Wilma was stunned into silence by what Suzi said. She wondered how she could have spent almost every day with her for twenty-five years and not predicted this. Recovering from the awkward moment, Wilma continued the conversation. "Suzi, all of us will get together next Tuesday when I get home. Let's meet at the church so we can talk things over with Pastor Charles, too. Will you do that?"

"Yeah, but I'm not going to let you girls talk me into anything I don't want to do. That's what usually happens, you know." Even though Suzi's emotions had settled down, her thinking remained unsettled. Wilma knew her best defense now was prayer. They agreed to meet the following Tuesday and said goodbye.

Wilma was disappointed she couldn't share all she had been through while visiting Jake, but she knew Suzi was in no condition to hear it. When Ray returned to the room, Wilma recounted her phone conversation. Ray gently and wisely reminded Wilma that in a crisis or in unusual circumstances, a person's true character would surface.

"Suzi has felt cheated in life and the lottery winnings have given her power to feel vindicated. Plain and simple."

"Plain and simple to you, Ray. But she's my friend. I don't think this is really who she is. It's like a switch has been flipped inside her."

"She has always been the one in the group to disagree. She never has seen things the way you and the others have." Ray never minced words when he wanted to make a point.

"I feel sorry for her, Ray. She lost her husband and her son. All she has left is a daughter-in-law who has been like a leech. Now this. I think Cecilia will play Suzi for all it's worth and get everything she can."

"I know you love her, but she will do what she must do. She will have the choice—just like you—as to what this money means. Maybe your example will have more effect than your words at this point." Ray's comments stabilized Wilma for the moment. "You have to keep focused on our future."

"I think I'll call the others and find out what they've been thinking," said Wilma.

Ray and Wilma engaged in a conversation about the individual impact of their common win. Ray believed a group decision was not realistic. He quoted scriptures from the Bible, stating chapter and verse, reminding Wilma that the love of money was the root of evil . . . that money had become THE GOD of this world, the standard that directed most behavior . . . that the decisions the girls would make, individually, would accord with their deepest moral fiber . . . that their personal consciences would be challenged by the money . . . and that, even though they had spent years together in church, this would surely put their beliefs to the test. He wondered whether they would need God anymore since they had the other god—money. Considering that she would soon part ways with her lifelong friends, he hoped Wilma would not be hurt. God had given them a new direction for their future and he was certain they would not waiver.

*   *   *

The summer season on Lake Michigan didn't really begin until the Fourth of July, so getting last-minute reservations at their favorite beach hotel for a weekend in June presented no difficulty for Margaret and Barbra Jean. Their families had grown close over the years; their children and grandchildren were about the same age. All three generations had remained in Cedar Lake, and school-related activities allowed them to spend more time together than they had with Wilma, Suzi, or Jean. It seemed natural to them to celebrate the lottery winnings together. After Saturday night dinner, Margaret and Barbra Jean had announced the winnings to their assembled families.

Margaret's middle-aged son Josh, born between sisters was the most vocal about the winnings, asking them to confirm the plans they had already made to live on The New World.

"I know the money could make our lives easier, but we still face the problems in our country that have caused us to decide to live on The New World. I really believe we are needed there. The opportunity to begin fresh as a Christian nation where money will not be the most important thing in our lives is the challenge before us. I believe God has allowed this in order to confront us with the truth in our own lives. He's asking us if we really believe in Him or the money."

Everyone was silent, contemplating his own motivation. Barbra Jean's youngest daughter spoke her thought aloud.

"But what if The New World is another plot to wipe out a large segment of the population, just like that flu shot did several years ago?"

She referred to a flu epidemic traced to free vaccinations for at-risk persons, including the elderly, pregnant women, and children. Within six months, 30% of the inoculees died. The causes of death were not the same in each case, but many believed the outbreak was a conspiracy to deal with the exponential growth of a government-dependent segment of the population. This and similar events caused a growing mistrust of government.

Their conversation lasted well into the night. These two families had lived upstanding lives in their community. They were people of faith who believed their personal relationship with God sustained them. At the end of a very long evening, they agreed they would not allow the money to change them—and the only way that would be possible would be to not keep it. As for its purpose, they decided to ask God's direction.

*   *   *

Ray and Wilma attended the two hour presentation at the Community Center in Burnham, designed as an orientation for the citizens of The New World. They agreed, had God not orchestrated the events of the week they would be excited by the prospect of this adventure. But in light of these happenings they were certain God had intervened.

CHAPTER 25

T uesday nights in Cedar Lake were normally calm, but the activity in the small parking lot at the Baptist church disrupted the quiet of this peaceful evening. Wilma had asked the girls and their families to attend this gathering where, in essence, the money was on trial. Pastor Charles agreed to mediate. The families greeted one another with their usual hugs. The mood was cheery, as they never lacked for words between them. Everyone knew the discussion would not end until they all knew what each planned to do with the money.

Pastor Charles stood at the foot of the elevated platform, togged in his customary jeans, polo, and sandals. He patiently waited until everyone arrived and took their seats. As they filed into the sanctuary, he silently observed their actions, watching for a reading on the outcome of this gathering. One by one, they settled into the pews. When the room was silent, he spoke.

"Let's invite God to join us."

Most of the attendees reverently bowed their heads until Pastor Charles finished his prayer. Then when he had everyone's attention, he briefly recounted what everyone knew: The spiritual condition of the country had rapidly declined to the point that living as a Christian had become difficult. The New World provided a solution to live as a cohesive society. It might not be the perfect solution, but America began in the same way—adventurous people with a dream who took a chance and sailed on treacherous waters with hope in their hearts. "We all know the outcome of that," he concluded. "America became the land of the brave and the home of the free."

Turning to the issue at hand, Pastor Charles continued, "So everyone must ask God for himself and be convinced that God is directing his path. There is no right or wrong decision, but we should all ponder where we would be the most effective in advancing the kingdom of heaven. Will it be on The New World? Or will it be here in Cedar Lake or somewhere else? This is an individual decision, not a group decision, because you are all different people with unique things to offer. God wants to use your life to benefit others.

"Oh, I suppose many of you are wishing this had never happened. Your lives were fine the way they were. This has changed everything. Everything, that is, except who you are on the inside. It's changed your circumstances, but it has not changed your character. I have confidence that all of you will choose well, since I have been acquainted with your character while you have been a part of this church and this community."

Wilma raised her hand and asked permission to speak first. "I have always thought we would grow old together," she chuckled, realizing that they were already old in some people's eyes. "I thought we would all continue to be friends on The New World just like we had been in Cedar Lake. But last week something happened to Ray, John, Jake, and me that caused us to change our minds. We saw the overwhelming needs of a nation left behind, yet hope came alive within us. We Americans have the equivalent of a Third World nation within our own borders. We send missionaries and aid outside our own country while we ignore the needs we have right here. God has shown us, as a family, this injustice, and we have vowed to help do something about it. I did not expect one week in Navajo Nation to change me like it has, but God has given us such clear direction that we see no other path. As far as our money goes, we'll use it to invest at John's direction, because it's going to take a lot of it to build what God has shown us.

"Ray and I are going to move to Navajo Nation as soon as we can and begin a new life there. We'll be moving in with Jake; he has plenty of room. I know, I know, he's had his problems, but we believe this is what we have prayed for in his life. He's made a 360-degree turnaround. He's discovered new purpose for his life. He's going to help us build a city with commerce to sustain the Navajo people. Never in our lives did we dream we would be a part of something like this, but I am certain of this direction because I get excited every time I think about it." She looked at Ray to question if he had anything to add. He smiled broadly and added an affirmative nod.

Margaret stood up next as spokesperson for her family. "Wilma and Ray, I am excited for you. That sounds wonderful," she began. Turning to the rest, she said, "As for us, we have decided that we don't want the money to change us, so we don't want to keep it. We would be tempted in so many ways, that all my children agree it's best to not even acknowledge it. I'll admit when we bought tickets every week, I never considered that we might win. It was just a game to me. But here we are, winners. Big winners! And we asked ourselves, 'Should that change us and the direction we were headed in?' We agreed, 'No.' We are all going to go live on The New World, because we believe we can help make it a better place. My son Josh is strong—physically and in his beliefs. He will make a good leader there.

"We don't know what we are facing, but we would rather be satisfied in helping forge the future than staying in Cedar Lake. Lord knows what's going to happen here, so we might as well risk the unknown up there. As for the money, we want it to go where it will be the most beneficial. Maybe it should go to Wilma and Ray because they are staying here and they have a worthy mission. They will need money since it is what guides this world . . ." She kept standing as her words trailed off, not sure of how to end her monologue.

After a few moments of silence, Barbra Jean stood up. "You all know that Margaret's family and mine have grown up together. Our families spent this past weekend together discussing what we should do and we arrived at the same conclusion. We don't want the money, either, and maybe you're right, Margaret. Maybe it should go to help Ray and Wilma in their plans. We won't need it on The New World." She looked at Margaret, nodded her head, and they both sat down, indicating their final verdict.

The room grew awkwardly silent as everyone waited for Suzi. She stood, wringing her hands and spurting her words erratically. "Okay, I guess I'm always the contrary one. I'm just going to be honest with all of you. I like the idea of having the money. I love all those handbags I've ordered. I even like the garden tiller and the juicer. It makes me feel secure and it gives me freedom that I have never felt before. I've always been a worrier and it's been hard to make ends meet. I'm afraid to go live on The New World. I only agreed to go because all of my friends were going and I thought if I stayed here, I would be lonely. But the money . . . well, it's changed everything. I'm going to stay here in Cedar Lake and keep the money. That is, most of it. I'm planning to give some of it away. Like to the church—Pastor Charles, I'm sure you could use some. And maybe some to Wilma and Ray. I guess I won't need all one hundred and three million. I don't have that long to live. But while I'm on earth, I'll be happier than I've been in a long time. I hope you girls don't hate me for this."

Wilma went to her and put her arm around her shoulder as Suzi slumped into the pew, weeping. "I'm sorry, Wilma," she blurted between sobs. "I love you girls, but this is what I have to do."

"It's okay, Suzi," said Wilma. "You heard what Pastor Charles said. We all have to make our own decisions and this is yours. We all still love you, too." The others came to her and surrounded her with reassuring hugs.

After a few minutes, Pastor Charles refocused the conversation by giving a progress report on Jean. "I've been at the hospital every day this past week with Jean. Things are critical for her. She's not ready to give up on life, so she has agreed to have her name on the list for an artificial heart. That means she will stay here in Cedar Lake and she will need money for her hospital bills. It will be expensive surgery, since it is still in the experimental stages. I've talked to her daughter, who couldn't be here tonight, and she wanted me to tell you of this decision. She says if Jean's health were better, she and her mom would choose to live the adventure on The New World."

Pastor Charles shifted to one foot, then the other, and continued. "In case you are wondering about me, I will be staying in Cedar Lake. I think there will be many people who are going to need this church once the Christians begin to go to The New World. I cannot imagine what this world will be like without the influence of Christians in politics, education, and business, but I am willing to stay, at least for a while, to see if spiritual guidance is needed.

"I have pondered this opportunity for Christians to live in a world guided by Christian morality, and this is what I think. Jesus told us that the Kingdom of God would not come with observation so that men will say 'here it is' or 'there it is,' because the Kingdom of God is within you. I interpret that to mean, unless the essence of God—that is, His Holy Spirit—dwells in the hearts of people and becomes the center and reason for their choices, then it will not matter where we live. We could be here in Cedar Lake or on The New World or Navajo Nation, but unless we do the will of God, which is to love Him and His ways with all of our hearts and love others as much as we love ourselves, then the physical location won't matter much." Pastor Charles bowed his head, giving time for his words to sink in.

He continued, "I am excited about your choices. They are diverse and I believe that is good. Two will stay in Cedar Lake, two will go to The New World and Wilma and Ray will go to Navajo Nation. And Suzi, I have confidence in you. I know about your hurts and pain and how you struggle with them, but I know you have always pursued God's ways. You'll be fine. God's influence on the earth and in the universe will go on in people. Right will prevail, and knowing that is what gives us hope.

Addressing the assemblage, the pastor continued, "This is the beginning of a new chapter for all of us, and when I say 'all of us,' I mean the world, too. We are on the brink of new opportunities that would not exist if we did not find ourselves in our current plight. Overcrowding, global climate change, moral decay . . . the list goes on. But God had fore-knowledge of this and He has a plan that will be carried out through people. That plan exists because He created us in His likeness, with amazing resilience, fortitude, and resourcefulness. Think of God and ask yourselves, 'How is it possible to be like Him?' Then look at Jesus and you will know. The lessons He taught and the principles He emphasized, not our circumstances, are the things that are eternal. Because of Him, we have strength to make a better world as we seek the way of love, not hate; contentment, not strife; peace, not fighting; patience, not intolerance: kindness, not hatefulness; good, not bad; truthfulness, not lying; tenderness, not roughness; and self-control, not indulgences. Circumstances throughout the ages have continued to change and the world has become much different, as we have sought to find solutions to our dilemmas. The internal things that have remained constant throughout the ages are the things that have sustained us in spite of our ever-changing circumstances. . . . and they will continue to sustain us throughout eternity."

Pastor Charles realized he was preaching a sermon, something he had not planned to do. "I guess when you get me in church, it's my cue. But seriously, please consider what I've said. Let's end this evening with prayer for God's blessing in each of your lives."

They all agreed they would continue to work at Corny's until their replacements were hired and trained. Mr. Bledshaw had been good to them and they wouldn't feel right about all leaving at the same time. The following months would be critical as they all closed this chapter in their lives and opened a new one.

Chapter 26

J ohn and Treeny attempted to resume their normal life in Chicago after their unusual trip to Arizona. It had been an epiphany, causing them to re-evaluate their priorities. They felt protective of the change within them and hoped their current obligations would not swallow it. John's focus was to handle the lottery winnings properly and seek wise investment opportunities. First on his *To Do* list: investigate investments into the Bank of The World. His network allowed him access to individuals who would guide him through the process. He would also be in constant contact with Jake and Leonard Bodie to assist them in developing a planning committee for the economic revival for the new city in Navajo Nation.

Treeny, inspired by the Native American colors in landscape and traditional garments, immediately began to design a line of clothing for babies, dedicating a percentage of the proceeds to fund an art museum in the new city. Both she and John battled the urge to be completely absorbed in their work. They knew it would be easy for old habits to take over if they didn't spend time together discussing the past week and how it would affect their future.

Treeny was in her design studio, deep in thought as she pulled swatches together, when her personal phone interrupted. Typically, John was the only one to call while she was at work, so she immediately grabbed it from her bag without noting the caller I.D.

"Hey, sweetheart," she cooed.

"I didn't know you thought of me so fondly."

"Oh! Hi, Jake. I thought you were John," she laughed.

Jake nervously laughed along with her.

"We were glad to be with you last week," she said graciously.

"It was good to be with both of you, too," he said, then cleared his throat. "Umm . . . you know I've never been very good at small talk, Treeny, so I'll get right down to the reason I've called."

"Sure, Jake. What is it?"

"It's Christina."

"Is she okay?"

"Yeah . . . yeah . . . she's beautiful. But I'm just afraid she might not be so good as time goes on. You know she was a shock to me. I mean, if the paternity test hadn't come back positive, I wouldn't have believed that she was mine. Who knew I had a daughter?" He cleared his throat again and paused.

Treeny gave him the courtesy of collecting his thoughts as she waited, holding her breath, anticipating the reason he might have called.

"You know our mom died when we were young and A-Dub stepped right into that role for John and me. I don't know what we would have done without her. Our dad did what he could for us, but if we wouldn't have had A-Dub and Uncle Ray, I don't know where we would be today. What I'm saying is, I don't want Christina to grow up without a mom. After last week, my life is making a turn, but I don't want nannies to raise Christina. And I know I can't do it by myself. I want her to have a mom."

Treeny's legs buckled as she grabbed onto a chair. A tear slid down her cheek as she recalled Christina's soft skin and sweet little voice. She attempted to choke back her emotions as she tried to stay in control. Finally, when she could no longer hold back, she began to sob. Jake waited a moment before he spoke again.

"Treeny, what I want to know is . . . well . . . will you be Christina's mom? You know, adopt her and raise her for me?"

Treeny tried to answer, but could only emit soft sobs over the phone. Jake didn't know what to do, so he just waited for her to speak.

"Oh, Jake, you don't how long I have waited to have a child. It's been my biggest heartache in life, to be childless. You don't know what John and I have been through. We've kept it kind of quiet. It was so personal, you know." Her sobbing took over again.

"Treeny, I couldn't help but notice how happy you and Christina were together. It was beautiful. I don't know all you and John have been through. I thought it had been a choice to not have kids. I was afraid you might say no. But Christina deserves to have a mom and you . . . well, you deserve a child."

"This is something that John and I will need to discuss, Jake, but I know our answer will be yes, a thousand times yes!"

Jake and Treeny ended their conversation, agreeing to work out the logistics over the next few days. *John, I've got to call John. No, it can't be on the phone. I need to see him face to face.* She grabbed her keys and her bag, telling her assistant that she would be leaving for personal reasons and would call to let her know when and if she would return today.

John gazed out at sparkling Lake Michigan from his 53rd floor office, as he often did during in-between times. He was distracted today. He had placed several calls and was waiting for answers before he continued with his next segment of business, so he didn't fight this distraction. A quiet knock on his closed office door brought him back to reality. His administrative assistant tentatively cracked open the door and poked her head into the room.

"Mr. Minda, I'm going out for lunch and I'm going right by your dry cleaners. Is there anything you would like me to drop off for you?"

"Um . . . yeah. I have a couple of jackets and a pair of pants in the closet. Go ahead and grab them. Thanks, by the way. I owe ya one."

"Don't worry about it, Mr. Minda. It's no trouble." She went to the large closet, but before she took the items of clothing from their hangers, her thorough nature compelled her to search the pockets. She found some change, a receipt for a lunch John should have turned in to Accounting, and a letter-sized envelope folded up in one of the jacket pockets. Emerging from the closet, she held the items out to John.

"Found them in your pockets."

He was accustomed to this ritual and casually asked her to put them on his desk. "I'm going by the accounting office," she said. "Want me to turn in this receipt for you?"

"Sure, sure," said John, a little aloof.

"How about this letter, Mr. Minda? It looks like you haven't opened it. Might be important, you know."

"Okay, I'll read it in a minute." He continued looking out over the lake. "Just put it on the desk."

"See you in about an hour." She closed the door as she left.

Treeny harbored no tolerance for traffic today. She was spilling over with excitement to talk with John about Christina and gave into an urge to lay on the horn, reminding the driver in front of her not to stop in the middle of the block.

"Why in heaven's name would you stop there? Other people are behind you. Just go!"

Soon she was able to ease into the left turn lane. Impatiently waiting for the traffic to clear, she entered the circular parking garage for the Hancock Towers. She orbited the corkscrew ramp all the way to the top, as all the lower floors were full. Dizzy by the time she reached the sun deck, Treeny was at her wit's end.

"It never fails when you are in a hurry. Nothing goes right."

A small voice deep in her soul interrupted her thoughts. "Quite the contrary. Everything is going right. The prayers of many have been answered. Your prayers, John's prayers, A-Dub's and Uncle Ray's prayers, Jake's prayers, Christina's dying mother's prayers, Christina's, and others you don't even know. What's a few more minutes?"

The words cut through her like a knife as if instant surgery removed the annoyance from her soul. Thankfulness took over as she wept . . . again. She imagined herself leaving the doctor's office with the news of having a child. Complete happiness that God had indeed answered her prayers. She was a blubbering mess, but John had seen her this way many times, so she felt no need to mask her emotions. Thoughts of her appearance while on the elevator did embarrass her, though. She didn't encounter anyone she knew, nor did anyone question her well-being, as she collected herself during the elevator ride.

Emerging from the elevator into the plush lobby of John's firm, she did feel the need to straighten herself. Her eyes darted about, purposing to avoid anyone she knew. She smiled weakly and waved to a couple of his office friends as she quickly found her way to John's office. The door was closed, typically a sign to stay out. She stood quietly for a moment before she tapped on the door and opened it in the same movement.

"Hi, hon," she chirped. She was taken by surprise to see John sitting at his desk, head in his hands. She could see from across the room that his eyes were red and watery. She closed the door behind her as she entered.

Walking straight over to him, she threw her arms around him and sighed, "Isn't it wonderful?"

He hugged her back as his shoulders heaved from scantly controlled sobs. Managing a whisper, he asked her, "How did you know?"

"Jake called me. Didn't he tell you?"

"Jake? What does Jake know about this?"

"Well, it is his daughter."

"It's a girl? How does he know?"

Treeny backed up for a moment, confused at John's response. "Of course it's a girl. You met her, too." Then Treeny noticed a handwritten letter on John's desk and, putting things together, realized they were talking about two different things.

"John, who's that letter from?"

"It's from Selena Owens. Jake's high school girlfriend. Pastor Charles gave it to me when I went to Cedar Lake. I was early to A-Dub's on Monday night so I stopped at the church. Pastor Charles said he had been saving this for the right moment."

"What's in the letter, John?"

"Forgiveness . . . for me. And a clean slate from the guilt I have carried since high school. I was so ashamed, I couldn't tell anyone, not even you. You know I don't keep secrets from you, but I thought I was an accessory to murder and come to find out I wasn't."

Treeny's eyes widened. "What are you talking about, John? Whose murder?" Her knees felt like jelly.

"Some people take abortion lightly, but I believe it is murder," said John.

"Whose abortion?"

"Selena Owens. But she didn't have the abortion. That means I have a child in the world somewhere." John bowed his head, ashamed he had not told Treeny. "Sit down for a minute. I need to tell you what happened."

Treeny and John sat on the sofa by the window as he recounted his one evening with Selena Owens and the outcome of that evening. The last he knew, they had agreed an abortion would be the best solution so he had given her money to fund it. Her plan was to disappear for a time and return when she worked things out, but she never returned to Cedar Lake. He handed Treeny the letter to read.

Dear John,

Usually when someone starts a letter with Dear John that means it's over. In this case, it's just beginning, for me that is. I have been talking with Pastor Charles about what has happened to me and he has helped me to see the future a little clearer. I was so scared when I found out I was pregnant that all I wanted was for it to go away. But Pastor Charles has helped me realize another way. Two wrongs don't make things right. Getting mad at Jake and sleeping with you was wrong but to murder an unborn baby would not make those things right. I would feel the guilt my whole life. God has forgiven me for the wrong things I've done and Pastor Charles helped me to make the decision to birth this child we have created. I don't know if I will be able to raise a baby or if I should allow another family to raise this child. I think the best thing for the child would be adoption. I'm not sure yet. I haven't included you in this decision because I know this is a decision I have to make alone. You and I are not in love and this didn't happen because of love. It was a mistake for us to be together that night and this is something I need to take care of by myself. Thank you for your financial help. I hope you don't mind that I have kept the money because I will need living expenses. I will be staying with a nice family that Pastor Charles has arranged for me. After that, I don't know what I'll do. All I know is that this is the right decision. I hope when this letter finds you that you will understand and that you too will find forgiveness.

Selena

Treeny reached out and took John's hand in hers. "Oh, John, I'm so sorry you didn't know sooner."

"Treeny, the important thing is that the child lived. It's not so important that it didn't live with me. The important thing is that I am not responsible for murder. I've tried to win God's forgiveness by doing all the right things."

"Do you want to try to find your child?" asked Treeny.

"No, I don't want to disrupt lives. That would be selfish of me. Don't you see, Treeny, it's not about the child. I'm sure God has provided it a wonderful life. I could never feel forgiven before, but now I do. It's as if it never happened. That weight has been lifted."

They both sat in silence for a while before John realized that Treeny had come to his office for a different reason.

"So, my love, what brings you to the Tower today? You couldn't have known this was going to happen."

"You aren't going to believe this. God's timing is uncanny." She looked deep into John's eyes. "If you say yes, we are going to have a child. A beautiful little girl." Treeny smiled as she let the news unfold serendipitously.

"What do you mean, if I say yes? How can that depend on me—and how can we know it will be a girl?"

"Jake called me and has asked if we will adopt Christina."

John grabbed Treeny in his arms and whispered, "Of course."

CHAPTER 27

The excitement of the news took a long while to subside. Looking out across the lake, John began to reveal another confession to Treeny. "This will be hard, but I have to tell Jake about more than Selena Owens. I hope he can forgive me, for all of it. I mean, I haven't done anything wrong, except not tell him a few things. For his own good," John began to justify his actions, then grappled with the truth. "But I made decisions without his full knowledge and they weren't my decisions to make. That makes it wrong."

"What kind of decisions?"

"I've lived in Jake's shadow my whole life and not realized how it has affected me," John said, ignoring the question for the moment. "He has always been the center of attention—by doing bad things. Maybe I would have felt different if he had been a better person, but his destructive daredevil behavior drew a lot of attention. I envied that attention—not the behavior, but the attention. I know it sounds ridiculous for a grown man to be jealous, but it developed when we were kids and I've never outgrown those feelings. Then he moved to Navajo Nation and I began to feel sorry for him. He was pitiful after that. I saw him becoming a drunk like our dad. He didn't care about anything, not even his money, so I started investing for him and not telling him about his profits. I made myself his beneficiary." John hung his head as he realized how this must sound to his innocent and trusting wife. "I could say a hundred things to justify what I've done, but in the end, I know I was wrong. My motivation was money, not concern for Jake."

"Johnnie, it doesn't sound like you've done him too wrong. I mean, you were making money for him, weren't you?"

"Yes, but I was afraid he would waste it like his first fortune from the NFL, so I simply didn't tell him about it. And, after he was gone, I would inherit it all. At the rate he was going, I didn't think he would last very long. Sure, it doesn't sound that bad, but my interest wasn't Jake, it was his money . . . and since we are all being honest, I need to admit some things. I just hope he forgives me and it doesn't affect his decision about us adopting Christina. I don't want to break your heart. I couldn't stand that." John came back to the sofa and sat beside Treeny. "As bad as all this is, it feels really good to have it out in the open."

"Johnnie, I love you no matter what and I forgive you for whatever wrong things you think you've done. Loving someone includes forgiving him, too. If Christina is to be a part of our lives, then God will work out the details." Treeny snuggled into John's chest, reassuring him.

"How do you do it?" asked John.

"Do what?"

"Make everything in the world seem okay. Your outlook is so optimistic."

"I dunno, Johnnie. I just know there are so many things I can't control, so I have to leave it up to God. There is always hope, no matter what."

"You're right. If we don't have hope, then we have nothing. We die. Hope is the thing that keeps us going always, in spite of all of our troubles. Hope looks at what might be instead of what is."

John and Treeny knew their future did not depend upon their decision or their desires alone. Neither Christina's future, nor Jake's, John and Treeny's, or A-Dub and Uncle Ray's, depended upon their dreams; it hinged upon how Jake would react to what John would tell him about his past investment practices. And *that*, they both knew, depended upon how quickly Jake would allow God to transform his heart.

Treeny broke the silence. "I know our future will not be the same as what our lives have been. Last week we were forever changed, but I think that was inevitable. The past few years have been a roller coaster of global change. It's been so hard to keep up with—and it's been exhausting. Oh, sure, markets have opened up like never before, but I think it's led to a lot of confusion. To some degree, the project of our new city is refreshing. It's about something sure. It's about the things we know and using that knowledge to benefit other people. Instead of continuing to press forward into the unknown, we are stopping, looking back, and giving a hand to help others catch up."

"One thing for sure, this will be change for Navajo Nation," said John.

"This is change they should have experienced a long time ago. This is sort of like going back and making things right for an entire nation. Like atonement for the sins of our forefathers. We've focused on trying to make things right with the slavery issues, but I don't believe we have ever tried to make things right with the Native American Indians."

"Oh, I think there has been an attempt with money. Native American Indians receive stipends, as well as other government subsidies."

"But when did we become a nation driven by money and not values?" mused Treeny.

"Treeny, my dear, we have always been a nation driven by money, even from the beginning. Men who sought economic opportunity founded Jamestown, our first settlement. That opportunity was about the wealth they stood to gain in a land of plenty. Plymouth, on the other hand, was established on principles and values. Religious freedom, not capital gain, was its origin. So the roots of our country were founded on these two ideals: greed versus God. It's been our story since the beginning and men like me have struggled with divided priorities ever since. I don't believe it's wrong to seek wealth, but when that driving force causes moral compromise, then it *is* wrong. I am thankful God has opened my eyes to see things in a new light. Now I know we don't need all that we have. Most of it has been to impress people anyway, and now that my priorities have changed, I don't feel the need to impress."

"You're right, Johnnie, we don't need most of what we have. Oh, it's been nice to live in luxury, but in all honesty, after our visit to Navajo Nation, I would feel guilty to continue to live this way. Don't get me wrong, I still want running water and electricity!" Treeny burst out laughing, easing the somber mood. She continued, "What do you think of moving my business out there? I mean, the Navajo women could sew the clothing. I could design and make the clothes at the same location rather than job out the sewing to other countries."

"That's a great idea, Treeny. You could even hire A-Dub to help you run things. You know she's been more than a bookkeeper at Corny's."

The phone buzzed, interrupting their conversation. "Mr. Minda, it's the call you have been waiting for."

"Thanks," he replied as he looked at Treeny and sighed. "I want to continue this conversation tonight, but this call is from the investors at The Bank of the World. It's about the proposal I've submitted."

Treeny, holding onto John's hand, stood to leave. She mimicked a phrase from an old movie she had used many times when his business conversations bored her. "A lady always knows when to leave." She kissed his hand and said, "Call you later."

John picked up his phone. "This is Mr. Minda."

"Hello Mr. Minda. This is Scott Bates. We received your proposal for economic development in America on Navajo Nation. Honestly, we are quite surprised to receive such a request from America. Normally our proposals come from Third World countries, not from prosperous nations like America."

"Yes, we realize that might be the case, Mr. Bates, but as our proposal pointed out, Navajo Nation is a separate nation with its own government."

"Yes, as you aptly stated, and that fact is not something one typically considers. But, as a sort of . . . well . . . a colony, in a sense, we thought perhaps America was taking care of its own."

John stiffened at his remark and intended to explain, but Mr. Bates continued.

"You have proven our belief to be incorrect with the photos and statistics you have presented. You have given us cause to carefully consider your proposal."

John's attitude did an about-face and he let his irritation fade as he exhaled. "Thank you, Mr. Bates. We are hoping for the finances that will enable Navajo Nation to build infrastructure, develop its own financial system, combat corruption, educate its people, and fund research, consultancy, and training."

"I believe you just stated the five key factors we feel necessary to assist economic development in underdeveloped countries," said Mr. Bates, smiling.

"I believe so," said John, also smiling. He and Mr. Bates had gotten off to a good start. They arranged to meet in Navajo Nation in three weeks to view the schematics designed by the urban planning committee. John knew that three weeks would be a near impossible task, but he also knew that Leonard Bodie expected a full presentation in six short weeks, including the finances. The exhilaration of the opportunity would fuel the fire.

He did a little dance around his office. This day was made for celebrating. Everything was going right. He thought he would call Jake while he was on a high note and picked up the receiver. *No sense dreading something that might be.* Jake would be surprised to hear from him so soon about the call from The Bank of the World.

In his home office, Jake had just ended a phone conversation with Leonard Bodie. He was mentally going over the conversation. They had agreed on their team for the urban planning committee; most of its members were selected from the Navajo Nation colleges. Jake insisted they take John's advice and head the committee with a renowned urban planning group from Chicago. Their expertise in land use and transportation planning would guide the team, while the Navajo Nation team members would influence the economic and social environments of the new city.

Jake had asked about Norman Lapahie and learned they were holding him without bond. His initial hearing was set for the following week. Jake agreed to take Bodie's advice about not attending Lapahie's hearing. Bodie encouraged Jake that even though he felt guilty about being involved in bootlegging, the trial was for murder, not bootlegging. He told Jake to accept God's pardon and move forward with the good he was about to be involved with in this new economic development.

Jake's phone rang, jolting him back to reality. "This is Jake," he said absentmindedly.

"Hey, it's John."

"Oh, hey, brother. Good to hear from you so soon. I guess you talked to Treeny?"

"Yep. You have made us very happy. Especially Treeny. She has wanted a child so badly and it just didn't seem like it was possible."

"Well, I'm concerned about Christina. I don't know how to be a mother and a father to her, and I don't think it's fair that she be raised by nannies. You know, an aunt and uncle raised us. We felt loved and they gave us a great home life. I know you and Treeny will do that for Christina."

"We will gladly adopt her, Jake."

There was a moment of awkward silence, but they quickly moved on to discussing the details of the adoption. They arranged planned visitations initially until Christina was familiar with John and Treeny. Jake felt that she had experienced enough disruptions over the past year. When the details were agreeable, John eased into the next piece of conversation about Selena Owens.

"Jake," he said, clearing his throat, "I have a confession to make to you."

"What kind of confession does a good guy need to make?"

"Hmm . . . that maybe that I'm not such a good guy. I've discovered some things about myself over the past few days and it's time to let some skeletons out of my closet."

Jake listened quietly as John began his admission of fraternal betrayal with Selena Owens and the outcome of his actions. He also admitted to Jake that he had blamed himself for Treeny not being able to carry a child all these years, fearing that infertility was God's punishment for the abortion. He tearfully read Selena's letter to Jake and confided his relief of this burden. He then asked Jake to forgive him.

"John, you have no idea how I have felt about you over the years. I was serious when I called you a good guy. That's how I have always looked at you. Me, on the other hand, well . . . that's another story. I believe I need to ask your forgiveness—for all the embarrassment I've brought on you and the family and the disrespect I've given."

John knew now was the time to wipe the slate clean and start over in this relationship with his only brother. He took a deep breath and proceeded boldly. "Jake, I forgive you from the bottom of my heart. I promise I won't hold anything against you. I will try to remember who you are today, not who you have been in the past. It might be hard at times, but please have patience with me."

Jake struggled to talk through his emotions. "Thanks, brother. I will try not to be such a jerk in the future. Most of all, I am committed to being sober and to staying in control of my actions. But, thanks, that means a lot."

John clenched his teeth as he continued, "Now, I need to confess something else to you. I have taken advantage of you financially. You didn't seem to care about your investments, so I've acted as though they were mine. In fact, I am beneficiary of all your money. I had you sign documents to that effect along with a ton of other stuff. I didn't think you would notice."

There was silence.

"Jake, I'm really not such a good guy and I need you to forgive me for this."

"John, are you sure we're twins? 'Cause I thought twins were on the same wavelength?"

"What are you talking about? Of course we're twins."

"You know my relationship with money. I believe it's to be used and you know I've used plenty of it. It's your thing to be concerned with planning and saving it. You would have disappointed me the most by not agreeing to adopt Christina—yet you jumped at the offer. If you had said no to adopting her, I would have questioned whether you were a good guy. But money? I am not now, nor have I ever been, about money. That is my least concern in life. So, forgive you? Gladly. But I might need to continue with an allowance; that is, if you're saying I still have money. I need an income now that I don't have the convenience store. But you can remain the beneficiary regarding the money . . . especially now that I know it will benefit Christina."

"So does that mean I'm forgiven?"

"Yes, of course you are," laughed Jake, and John joined in.

"For Selena, too?" asked John.

"Yes, for stealing my girlfriend, too," said Jake.

"We're going to have some good times together," said John.

"I think you're right," said Jake. "It feels good to have a fresh start and to have something in life to work toward. The adventure of building our new city is now our lifetime quest."

John reflected on his earlier conversation with Treeny about hope, and added with a smile, "And the adventure of serving God will last beyond that."

The conversation about The Bank of the World could wait. The connection of brother to brother, heart to heart, was more important today . . . as the two men, born the same day—and reborn the same day—shared stories of their dreams and miraculous deliverance from their selfish lives.

"LET ME TELL YOU WHY YOU ARE HERE.
YOU'RE HERE TO BE SALT-SEASONING
THAT BRINGS OUT THE GOD-FLAVORS OF THIS EARTH.
IF YOU LOSE YOUR SALTINESS,
HOW WILL PEOPLE TASTE GODLINESS?"
JESUS

THE MESSAGE
THE BIBLE IN CONTEMPORARY LANGUAGE

About the Author

Frieda Dowler, mid-western hairstylist, fuses ordinary people's extraordinary stories into snapshots of imagined unfolding adventures in published works; The New World Kingdom of Heaven, and New Money for an Old America. As wife, mother, daughter and business owner she intertwines creativity with responsibility.